GOSPEL ZERO

RECLAIMING THE RADICAL MESSAGE OF GRACE

ANDREW FARLEY
JOHN LYNCH

REGNERY
FAITH

Regnery Faith books may be purchased in bulk at special discounts for sales promotion, corporate gifts, fund-raising, or educational purposes. Special editions can also be created to specifications. For details, contact the Special Sales Department, Regnery Faith, 307 West 36th Street, 11th Floor, New York, NY 10018 or info@skyhorsepublishing.com.

Andrew Farley is represented by Don Gates @ The Gates Group, www.the-gates-group.com.

Regnery Faith is an imprint of Skyhorse Publishing, Inc.®, a Delaware corporation.

Visit our website at www.regnery.com.
Please follow our publisher Tony Lyons on Instagram @tonylyonsisuncertain.

10 9 8 7 6 5 4 3 2 1

Library of Congress Cataloging-in-Publication Data is available on file.

Cover design by Hope Certalic

Print ISBN: 978-1-5107-8236-5
Ebook ISBN: 978-1-5107-8237-2

Printed in the United States of America

To you, the reader,

Welcome! You've just stepped into something different—something you've always suspected but maybe couldn't quite put into words. This book is for those longing to break free from the noise and chaos of the world and dive into the raw, untamed richness of life with Jesus. If you've ever felt like you were the only one, you're not alone. As you turn these pages—written for the curious and the hopeful—may God light your path, affirm who you truly are, and remind you of His boundless grace. Get ready to laugh (yes, laugh!), cry, and wrestle with the messy beauty of grace. This is an adventure like no other. Once you see the truth, there's no going back!

CONTENTS

PART 3: THE ART OF ETERNAL AMNESTY

PART 4: DIVINE ENTWINE

FOREWORD

Some books educate. Some books entertain. And then there are rare treasures that manage to do both while completely revolutionizing the way we think about God and faith. *Gospel Zero* is one of those books.

Imagine if C.S. Lewis's *The Screwtape Letters* had a snarky cousin who teamed up with *The Shack* for a wild road trip through the modern church. That's *Gospel Zero*. It's a bold, witty, and wildly creative series of letters, penned in the voices of modern-day apostles, who pull no punches as they dissect lifeless religiosity and point us back to the singular beauty of Jesus Christ. The result? A spiritual masterpiece that's as hilarious as it is profound, as convincing as it is liberating.

Gospel Zero showcases God's grace with a masterful fusion of Andrew Farley's profound biblical insights and John Lynch's captivating wit and charm. This book delivers a compelling and eye-opening perspective on how the New Testament writers might perceive the modern church. *Gospel Zero* is a must-read that will inspire and challenge you to experience God's love in a transformative new light. It is destined to become a timeless classic that will resonate with Christians around the globe for generations.

But let me explain why this book stands out in such a crowded field. Andrew Farley brings the theological weight. His deep dives into Scripture uncover rich truths that shake the foundations of tired traditions and make the grace of God leap off the page. His insights aren't just profound; they're life-altering, exposing the cracks in legalistic mindsets and pointing us to the freedom that Christ died to give us. And then there's John Lynch. What can I say? The man is a comedic genius with a heart for truth. His turns of phrase are razor-sharp, his humor disarming, and his perspective so fresh that you'll find yourself laughing and nodding along, even as he calls out the contradictions in modern religiosity.

Together, these two authors create an alchemy of wisdom and wit that's unlike anything else you've read. Their partnership in this book is a revelation in itself—a blend of profound theology and side-splitting humor that will make you think, laugh, and occasionally wince (in the best possible way).

These letters, voiced by the fictional apostles Andronicus and Johannes, take us on a journey through the modern church as if seen through the eyes of ancient wisdom. It's like eavesdropping on a scathing yet redemptive apostolic intervention—a dramatic rebuke wrapped in grace and delivered with humor. Every page brims with a biting wit that exposes the pitfalls of performance-based religion while pointing us back to the simplicity of Christ.

Reading *Gospel Zero* feels like watching a play unfold—equal parts drama, satire, and heartfelt truth. It's Galatians amplified, with the humor dialed up and the stakes laid bare. And yet, through it all, the message is one of hope. These imagined letters remind us that we are fully forgiven, perfectly loved, and free to live as God's beloved children.

Whether you've been weighed down by guilt or are simply curious about the kind of freedom the Gospel promises, this book is for you. It's for anyone ready to laugh, cry, and rediscover the joy of walking in God's grace. Prepare yourself for a spiritual journey unlike any other. Dive in with an open heart and a ready laugh—you're in for a transformative, unforgettable ride.

BART Millard
singer/songwriter for MercyMe

the message is one I have. I have imagined letters [illegible] that we are fully forgiven, perfectly loved, and free to live as God's beloved children.

Whether you're just beginning to explore faith or are simply curious about the kind of freedom the Gospel promises, this book is for you. It's for anyone ready to be honest and to discover the joy of walking in God's grace. Prepare yourself [illegible], encouraged, and drawn closer to God [illegible] transformative [illegible].

BART Millard
Lead singer of MercyMe

INTRODUCTION

Imagine this: Lloyd, a devout churchgoer, is dosed with a truth serum. Lloyd has clocked in at every Bible study, led a couple of small groups, and even survived a few mission trips. He's memorized Scripture and can quote sermons like they're the latest box office hits.

With the serum in full swing, an interviewer moves in like a hawk on a mouse. "So, Lloyd, how's church working out for you? The teachings, the sermons—how's it all impacting your life?"

Lloyd, suddenly without a filter, zeroes in on the interviewer's incessant pen-clicking. "Can you quit with that clicking? It's enough to drive anyone mad."

Caught off guard, the interviewer stammers, "Uh, sure. So, tell me about your church experience."

Taking a deep breath, Lloyd starts. "You want the real scoop on how this whole church thing's been going for me. My experience in the Christian community." He recounts over thirty years of faith, starting with a transformative summer camp in upstate New York.

Lloyd speaks of his initial fervor: avid Bible reading, a profound connection with Jesus, and a newfound confidence and purpose.

"I felt so alive. I knew I was a different person," Lloyd reminisces about those early days of freedom and joy.

But then, the narrative shifts. What began as messages of unconditional love and acceptance morphed into sermons on personal failings and moral obligations. "I started hearing about what I should be doing, what a failure I was," Lloyd recalls, noting the stark contrast to his early, liberating faith. The absence of messages purely about Christ's love, untainted by moral prerequisites, began to gnaw at him. Joy gave way to a sense of duty and obligation.

"There's an unspoken code . . . Don't mess up, don't trust your gut, get with the program, and for heaven's sake, don't think outside the box," he says, highlighting the pressure to conform and the inevitable guilt of falling short.

At one point, Lloyd breaks his flow to snap at the interviewer again about the pen-clicking. "Seriously, stop that!"

Lloyd's story is a struggle, not just with faith, but with his identity as a Christian. He grapples with the fear of hypocrisy and the exhausting effort to appear as the "good person" he's been told to be. He concludes, "Honestly, I'm worn out from all this striving and falling short. What happened to simply feeling loved and accepted for who I am?"

"Can I leave now?" he sighs, capturing the weariness of playing the role of "perfect Christian," longing for the freedom and joy that once defined his relationship with God.

As the serum's effects wear off, Lloyd—and many others like him—return to the superficial reassurance of being "fine," despite the underlying turmoil fueled by a constant sense of inadequacy.

Modern Christianity and the Pursuit of Self-Improvement

The modern church's legalism is so thick, you'd need a spiritual jackhammer to break through it. Our critique isn't a whisper in the halls of theology but a shout from the rooftops, echoing the frustration and disillusionment of countless believers bogged down by the quagmire of "do more, try harder" Christianity.

In the trenches of this spiritual battlefield, the concept of resting in Christ seems as alien as a third arm. The modern religious mantra implies that the Christian life is akin to an uphill battle in hurricane-force winds. Funny, isn't it? It's not like anyone can boast, "Through enough self-discipline, I've actually stopped sinning." Said no one, ever.

The mixing of law and grace in today's preaching is about as harmonious as oil and water. It's a concoction so foul, it makes telemarketers, rickets, and smog seem appealing by comparison. The legalism infusing much of modern teaching insists on partial adherence to outdated mandates, as if Jesus hadn't fulfilled the Law once and for all. Looking to the Old Testament law for Christian living advice is like ordering take-out from a place that shut down years ago.

The Christian world is rife with contradictions and impossibilities. We're told to get closer to God, as if He were a distant relative rather than the indwelling presence of the Holy Spirit. Getting closer to Jesus is about as achievable as getting closer to your own shadow. Yet, this doesn't stop the relentless treadmill of trying to achieve a proximity to God that is already ours in Christ.

The identity crisis among believers is perhaps the most tragic. The term "saved sinner" is an oxymoron that perfectly encapsulates the confusion—it's like describing a root canal as hilarious. This mixed-up identity leaves believers stuck in a loop of spiritual schizophrenia, never fully embracing the new creation they are in Christ.

Forgiveness these days feels like a limited-time deal that keeps needing renewal, as if God's got an expiration date. This fundamentally undermines Jesus's sacrifice on the cross. If Jesus died once and for all our sins, how many times does He need to die to get you to stop asking for His forgiveness? The implication that we are not fully forgiven leads to a life of spiritual groveling, as if we could somehow repay Christ for the infinite cost of our redemption.

Grace, the very heart of the Gospel, is portrayed as a delicate balance rather than the overwhelming flood that it truly is. The notion that we could have too much grace is as ludicrous as fearing an excess of wholesomeness. Grace balanced with anything else is no longer grace. Yet, this hasn't stopped the church from trying to dilute the potency of grace with legalistic additives, as if it were a dangerous substance that needed to be handled with care.

In a world obsessed with self-improvement and spiritual disciplines, the message of the Gospel stands out as a radical departure. Thinking we can discipline our way to holiness is as absurd as trying to shed pounds by reciting haikus. And yet, the treadmill of spiritual disciplines continues to run, powered by the guilt and shame of never doing enough.

As a result, we find believers trapped in routines devoid of heart or passion. Reading the Bible or praying because you ought to is like breathing air out of dutiful obligation. This robotic devotion is worlds away from the vibrant, soul-stirring relationship Scripture invites us into. Who is more delightful to encounter than one who is joyfully obedient to Jesus because they are trusting His grace? Yet these are few and far between.

The Letters: A Radical Call to Grace

Imagine a series of letters penned by modern apostles, Andronicus and Johannes—figures who embody the wisdom and zeal of their biblical counterparts yet speak into our present reality with startling clarity. These letters serve as a bridge, connecting the timeless truths of the Gospel with the unique challenges and opportunities facing today's church.

What if these apostles strolled through our modern churches, eyes wide at the contradictions woven into our faith communities? What messages would they convey to us, using the digital parchment of our era? Through their eyes, we'll explore how the vibrancy of early Christian faith can illuminate our path, guiding and inspiring us toward a fuller understanding of grace and our identity in Christ.

This is not merely a thought experiment; it's an invitation to a radical dialogue—a call to reconsider our assumptions and realign our practices with the heart of the Gospel. As Andronicus and Johannes share their observations, they will undoubtedly offer both commendation and critique, blending encouragement with sharp admonishment where we've strayed from our first love. Their letters—though imagined—will hit hard, pushing us to tear down the walls of legalism and reclaim the joyous freedom of living as God's beloved children.

May their words provoke, comfort, and ultimately guide us back to the essence of what it means to know Christ in a world hungry for authentic, transformative grace. Welcome to a conversation centuries in the making, yet as urgent as our next breath.

Now, dive into the letters and let Andronicus and Johannes guide you through a transformative journey. Prepare to be challenged, inspired, and refreshed as we uncover the pure, unadulterated message of grace that can reset our understanding of Christianity and revolutionize our whole experience with God.

PART 1

COVENANTAL CRESCENDO

AN ESSENTIAL ELIXIR

To the Faded Faithful Who Forget Freedom's Feel:

It's a crying shame, a real head-scratcher, that the bedrock of our faith is getting less airtime in our sacred halls than a silent film in a blockbuster cinema.

Here we stand, the modern church, afflicted with a spiritual amnesia, like the grace woven by Jesus has vanished quicker than a politician's campaign promises. Echoing those "foolish Galatians," who began the right way but then got distracted by human effort (Galatians 3:3), we're on the brink of swapping freedom for the fetters of elbow grease spirituality, with our "do more, try harder" mentality to "get closer" to God and rid ourselves of the so-called "idols" in our supposedly wicked hearts. Paul's letter to the Galatians wasn't just an ancient rant—it was a divine wake-up call, reminding us that life in the Spirit beats stone-chiseled commandments and gutting it out any day.

God's new way of grace isn't just a tweak to an old contract; it's a game-changer. Hebrews 8:6 doesn't mince words as it announces "a better covenant" with "better promises," and neither did Jesus as He laid down His life, not just flipping the script but completely rewriting the playbook of our relationship with God. The cross isn't just a historical milestone; it's the pivot point of eternity, swapping the outdated for an upgrade, etched not on tablets but on our hearts, with Jesus's own blood as the ink.

So why, oh enlightened ones, do we gaze longingly back at the chains of our own Egypt when the promised land of Christ's freedom is right under our noses? Why do we opt for the shadow puppetry of law when the reality is standing right in front of us, in 3D, no glasses required? Our churches, meant to be greenhouses of grace, often morph into grim courthouses, complete with a law-touting Pharisee banging the gavel of guilt. Talk about missing the point—this is like trying to use a map of Middle-earth to navigate across Europe.

Paul's not-so-subtle nudge in Galatians to live by the Spirit and chuck the yoke of the law overboard is as relevant as your morning coffee. The way of God's grace isn't a get-out-of-jail-free card for chaos; it's an invitation to dance to the beat of a higher law—the law of love. It's about heart over habit, identity over ordinance, Spirit-led living over rule-following drudgery.

We are often caught measuring our spiritual pulse with the outdated apparatus of religious rituals rather than the vibrant presence of love, joy, peace, and the whole fruit basket of the Spirit. Let's have a collective "aha!" moment: being led by the Spirit means we've officially broken up with the Law—it's time to get over it already. This isn't just some doctrinal footnote; it's the headline news that should be blaring through every aspect of our church life.

As we gaze into the mirror of God's Word, let's not be the forgetful ones who stroll away, oblivious to their own reflection. The New

Covenant shows us our true faces—not marred by the law but marked by Christ's resurrection life, sanctified, redeemed, beloved. It's high time our sermons and songs echo this truth, not celebrating our legal liabilities but our royal righteousness in Christ.

Let this letter be more than a nudge—let it be a rallying cry for the church to rediscover the heart of the Gospel. May we ditch the dusty robes of legalism and fully suit up in God's grace. For it's in this climate of spiritual freedom that we truly flourish, bearing fruit that will turn heads and hearts toward the radiant glory of Christ. The world needs to see what it looks like to truly live.

Yours in the endless adventure of grace,
Andronicus and Johannes

THE DANCING DUO

To the Weary Wanderers Wanting Warmth:

We're reaching out to highlight an oversight that seems to be making the rounds in your hallowed halls. Yes, we're talking about that age-old classic—the riveting saga of grace versus law—a narrative so gripping, yet glossed over faster than a guilty glance at a speeding ticket in the rush to moralize our pews into neat, guilt-laden rows.

In our current epoch, where the siren song of "lawfulness" is more alluring than ever, many have merrily marched down the path not to righteousness but to an existence crushed under the sheer weight of rules. But Scripture, in all its wisdom, couldn't be clearer: sticking to the Law—whether in bits or the whole—is like signing up for sin's permanent residency program with zero perks:

- "The Law came in so that the transgression would *increase*" (Romans 5:20)
- "the sinful passions, which were *aroused* by the Law" (Romans 7:5)

- "for *apart* from the Law sin is dead" (Romans 7:8)
- "the power of sin *is* the law" (1 Corinthians 15:56)

Yet, in a twist that would make any soap opera proud, our pulpits champion a cherry-picked buffet of the Law—from the sacred art of tithing to the holy observance of rest days, not to mention the timeless classics against fibbing, thievery, and the lustful eyeing of your neighbor's new chariot.

Let's be crystal clear: the Law, with its Ten Golden Hits, isn't your stairway to heaven—it's more like a flashing neon sign screaming "mess-up alert," leading you straight to the trapdoor of failure. And 2 Corinthians 3:7–9 is quite theatrical about this as it refers to the Big Ten "engraved on stones" as a "ministry of condemnation" and a "ministry of death."

This might ruffle some feathers, maybe even sound scandalous, but it's Gospel 101, folks. Opting to live under any slice of the Law is like RSVPing to your own perpetual pity party. The Apostle Paul illustrates this with his "coveting of every kind" conundrum under the Law's unflinching gaze (Romans 7:8). Yep, Paul was stuck under "Thou Shall Not Covet" (another one of those Ten Golden Hits) and couldn't stop eyeing his neighbor's donkey like it was the newest iPhone drop.

It's an all-or-nothing game with the Law. James and Galatians are adamant about this! Handpicking from the Law is a profound misread of its purpose:

- "For whoever keeps the whole law and yet stumbles in *one point*, he has become guilty of *all*." (James 2:10)

- "for it is written, 'Cursed is everyone who does not abide by *all things* written in the book of the law, to perform them.'" (Galatians 3:10b)

The Law, in all its impossible-to-achieve glory, was meant to bring us to our knees—not in despair, but in a leap of faith toward the grace found in Christ.

Friends, we've officially broken up with the Law, courtesy of Christ, to be in an exclusive relationship with God. Digging up the Law is like sliding into your ex's DMs—spiritually cringe-worthy at best. The Law still stands as a testament to divine holiness, but in Christ, we've ghosted the Law for a life led by the Spirit.

This whole debate about the Law's role in our lives should really be over by now. The Gospel is simplicity itself: liberated from the Law to bask in the Spirit, swaying to the rhythm of grace and love in Christ. The New Testament, with its spiritual jazz, isn't laying down a new law but riffing on the life of the Spirit within us.

In Christ, we hit the jackpot. The Law has been fulfilled not by us ticking off its demands but through His sacrifice. And now the call to love as He loves isn't a drag; it's the freedom of living in stereo, powered by the Spirit.

So why, oh why, are we sitting through a rerun of *The Law's Greatest Hits* in our congregations? Must we cling to a burden even our spiritual ancestors couldn't shoulder? Let's not be the sequel to the foolish Galatians, hoodwinked by a repeat of legalism.

We implore you, siblings in spirit, to dive back into the Scriptures, to immerse yourselves in the vast ocean of freedom Christ has unlocked for us. Let's shed the weight of legalism and waltz in the glorious liberty of grace and truth. May our lives be a rave review of the Spirit's transformative power, not a tribute band to the Law we've bid adieu.

Here's to not resuscitating a bygone covenant but living out loud in a covenant of the Spirit, grooving to His hit parade of love, joy, peace, and all that jazz. Christ dropped the ultimate liberation album; let's crank it up and refuse to hit the "legalism" station ever again. Because, honestly, why settle for yesterday's noise when we've got the Spirit's anthem of freedom?

In the boundless love of Christ,
Andronicus and Johannes, your fellow freedom fighters

THE VERDICT

To the Thirsty Theologians and Their Suffering Students:

The Law is that overzealous gym teacher, so fixated on laps that they forgot the sheer joy of the game. And keeping up with its endless list of do's and don'ts? Tougher than chewing on a two-dollar steak cooked to shoe leather. Engaging with the Law is like stepping into spiritual quicksand, each attempt to adhere to its standards dragging you further into the pit of guilt.

Haven't you ever felt a peculiar urge to do the precise opposite of a given directive? Exhibit A: the "Keep Off the Grass" sign. Nothing transforms a law-abiding citizen into a midnight rebel—an after-hours anarchist—faster than a forbidding plaque.

But fear not, for this narrative does not end in despair. Jesus did not come to Earth and offer the ultimate sacrifice only to then say, "Carry on sweating the minutia." No, He orchestrated the seismic shift from "You can't sit with us" to "VIP access for all who believe."

Trying to mingle law and grace? About as useful as brewing tea in a chocolate teapot—appealing in theory, but utterly disastrous in practice.

You are cordially invited to dine eternally at the Table of Grace, where attire of sackcloth and ashes is decidedly passé. You're now a proud member of the "Christ in Me" club. Your membership benefits include joy that defies expression, peace that stands unassailable, and an endless reservoir of God's love, rendering all alternatives as mere imitations.

Never forget that the Law simply serves as the ultimate "I told you so," designed to illustrate that the pursuit of righteousness through checkbox spirituality is doomed to failure. The Law's role? To guide us to Grace's doorstep, then vanish like a magician, leaving us both stunned and set free.

However, it seems we possess a penchant for reviving the Law, dressing it in contemporary garb, and parading it as if it remains the belle of the ball. The outcome? A cadre of so-called experts acing their doctrinal examinations while fundamentally misunderstanding Grace 101.

Indeed, grace appears too generous to be true, particularly to those schooled in the dogma of spiritual self-flagellation. So, the Law emerges as that high-maintenance companion, keen on highlighting every flaw without offering assistance. It's the spiritual equivalent of tripping over a "Watch Your Step" sign—ironic and painfully obvious.

Then there's Augustine, who had an interesting perspective on forbidden things. He might say something like, "You think that fruit is off-limits? Watch what happens next." He pointed out that the excitement often comes not from the fruit itself (because honestly, who genuinely gets excited about figs?), but from the act of breaking the rules and doing something that's not allowed. The real thrill is in the rebellion.

Enter Romans 7:5 and 7:8, where Paul divulges how the Law inadvertently served as a magnet for sin.

- "the sinful passions, which were aroused by the Law" (Romans 7:5)
- "sin, taking opportunity through the commandment" (Romans 7:8)

In essence, the Law didn't merely fail to deter sin; it offered us a sin-inducing environment of stifling rules. Fortunately, Romans 6:14 flips the script: "For sin shall no longer be your master, because you are not under the law, but under grace." Suddenly, we find ourselves not dodging God's retribution for each misstep but basking in the lavish spread of grace, where our foibles are met with mercy rather than tallying on a heavenly scorecard.

Living under the Law is akin to dancing in mismatched shoes—awkward, exhausting, and guaranteed to end in a stumble. Grace, however, is the grand ballroom where every misstep—regardless of its clumsiness—is met with applause, and each fall is cushioned by open arms.

In an atmosphere stifled by rule adherence, the Gospel of grace turns the narrative upside down. Here we are, at history's crossroads, choosing between the dusty dead-end of legalism or the liberating highway of grace.

The verdict is unanimous: Grace triumphs, unequivocally and magnificently.

Feeling a great sense of hope,
Andronicus and Johannes

HISTORY'S PIVOT

To the Critics of the Cross and to the Doubtful Dreamers in the Desert:

We're jotting down these words to catapult our minds back to a truth as old as time—yet as elusive as that one sock you swear your dryer ate. We're talking about the cross, folks—the real game-changer, the ultimate plot twist in the saga of humanity.

Let's dive into the often bewildering, yet fascinating realm of Scripture. Take, for instance, Hebrews 9:17, with its talk of covenants kicking in post-mortem and only being valid "when men are dead, for it is never in force while the one who made it lives." Or consider Jesus, over a cozy dinner, chatting about "the new covenant in My blood" (Luke 22:20). These snippets shift the spotlight from the cozy manger to the brutal cross—the true dividing line of history, marking the dawn of the New Testament era.

As we flip through the sacred pages, just before Matthew 1, there's a billboard titled "THE NEW TESTAMENT." Caution! It's misleading. The real show begins not with Jesus's baby shower but with the curtain call of Jesus's earthly visit (yeah, the cross). This isn't just a theological tidbit; it's the decoder ring for understanding Jesus's most puzzling one-liners: Cut off your hand. Pluck out your eye. Sell everything. Be perfect like God.

Galatians reminds us that Jesus popped up under the Old Covenant's watch to guide those trapped in its web to freedom. Yes, He was "born of a woman, born under the Law, so that He might redeem those who were under the Law" (Galatians 4:4–5). His ministry, a thrilling adventure set against the backdrop of Old Covenant norms, provides crucial context for His interactions and teachings.

Jesus, addressing a crowd with a strong penchant for the Law, doled out commands that seemed to demand the impossible. Think of it as the Law on steroids—plucking out eyes, chopping off hands (Matthew 5:29–30), and the Herculean task of being as perfect as God (Matthew 5:48).

Then, the plot thickens with Jesus's last supper cameo, foreshadowing the transition from the Law's iron grip to the liberating embrace of His grace (Luke 22:20). "The new covenant in my blood," He called it. Key word: blood (not birth). The New Covenant kicks off at His death, not at His baby shower.

Seeing the cross as the plot's pivot point sharpens Jesus's entire mission. His stern warnings and sky-high standards weren't about crafting a new legalism but revealing our dire need for a Savior.

Jesus's tough love was aimed at the proud, showcasing the Law's unattainable bar and humanity's thirst for grace. Spotting the cross as the narrative's fulcrum frees us from thinking there's a new set of spiritual hoops to jump through.

Fast forward, and we meet Jesus's one-of-a-kind priesthood—a total break from the old Levitical playbook. This isn't just a changing of the guard but a whole new ballgame, signaling grace's debut on the world stage.

Hebrews 7:12 doesn't beat around the bush—the priesthood's overhaul demands a law swap. Jesus, hailing from Judah (not Levi), underscores the old system's obsolescence, urging us to ditch the worn-out for the brand-spanking-new.

Blending Old and New Covenant elements is as futile as mixing oil and water. So, the choice before us couldn't be starker: cling to the old, with its rituals and regulations, or leap into the New Covenant's open arms, where grace, forgiveness, and a direct hotline to God await.

The New Covenant isn't just a tweak to the Old—it's a whole new paradigm, where grace reigns and direct access to God is our prized possession.

As we journey forward, let's not slide back into the old ways. Christ, our eternal High Priest, beckons us into a realm where grace abounds, the Law is fulfilled, and our identities are defined by His death and resurrection.

So, here's to ditching the old for the new. May our letter not just tickle your intellect but stir your soul to embrace the freedom of the New Covenant—a life where grace, not effort, wins the day.

Yours in the relentless pursuit of liberty,
Andronicus and Johannes

MISSION IMPOSSIBLE

To the Pilgrims of the Pulpit and the Battered Believers at the Barricades:

In the grand circus of Christian discourse, there's a subset of teachings—a whirlwind of divine demands so sky-high they make Cirque du Soleil look like child's play. Here we are, pen trembling, hearts caught between despair and hope, ready to throw a glaring spotlight on the Sermon on the Mount—a scriptural gem that shines and confounds all at once.

Picture a standard so divine, so wildly out of reach, that trying to meet it with sheer grit is like scaling Everest in flip-flops. Jesus, in His infinite wisdom, didn't just set the bar high—He rocketed it into the stratosphere, daring His listeners to pull off a mission more impossible than Tom Cruise could dream of. Here's a highlight reel of His Moses 2.0: Cut off your hand if you sin. Yank out your eye if it leads you astray. Out-righteous the Pharisees. Anger equals murder. Looking with lust equals adultery. Give money to anyone who asks. Let people beat you up. Pray for the guy who slashed your tires. Hide your fasting and giving. Oh, and be perfect—like God.

Jesus's commands in Matthew 5–7 weren't meant to kick off a self-mutilation club or inspire vows of poverty. They scream one glaring truth: The standard is so sky-high that grace isn't just an accessory—it's your only parachute.

Yet, in today's world, we declaw these teachings, sanding down their rough edges, or worse—shoving them aside for something more "user-friendly." Enter the age of Selective Hearing Syndrome. This results in "covenantal confusion," where the lines blur between the old and the new, and the gleaming bridge from law to grace that Christ built gets lost in the fog of denial.

When Jesus dropped this bombshell sermon, He wasn't dishing out self-help tips for better living. He was unveiling the absurdity of trying to achieve righteousness through DIY holiness. To His Jewish audience, swimming in law and tradition, He served up a reality check that would give anyone vertigo: trying to reach heart-level purity through rule-following was like trying to stop a train with a toothpick.

This sermon isn't a bludgeon to beat us into submission—it's a flashing sign pointing out our own spiritual bankruptcy. It's the Mount Everest of moral demands, showing us the impossible gap between God's perfection and our pitiful best efforts (Romans 3:23; James 2:10). Jesus's sky-high standards were the ultimate GPS redirect, forcing His listeners toward the only exit: the New Covenant, which fulfilled the Law in ways that human sweat and tears never could. Under this new paradigm, grace is the name of the game, and our only move is to accept it, not strive for it (Ephesians 2:8–9).

Jesus was talking to folks under the Old Covenant, and His words were a mirror reflecting just how hopeless the old system was. It wasn't about keeping the Law; it was about recognizing our desperate need for a Savior. The Law's 613 demands weren't a finish line—they were a brick wall meant to make us cry uncle. And that's the point of Jesus's killer sermon—to leave anyone broke, busted, and knowing we need a rescue.

Flash forward to today, and we're right back where the Galatians stood—staring at a crossroads. We're called to step into the freedom Christ has secured for us, not to slap the shackles of legalism back on (Galatians 5:1). Our job? Preach the whole truth—don't sugarcoat the Sermon on the Mount, but use it to showcase the glory of grace. Let's not downplay the impossibly high standard Jesus set. He wasn't asking for our "best effort."

No, let's resist the urge to dumb down His teachings and make them more palatable. Instead, let's let the Sermon's jaw-dropping demands propel us straight into the loving arms of God's grace (Romans 11:6). Because, in the end, Jesus didn't raise the bar just to trip us up—He obliterated the whole idea of "bars" altogether for those who believe. It's all grace, start to finish.

Showcasing the perfect and impossible standard so you opt out,
Andronicus and Johannes

DISCERNING THE DIFFERENCE

To the Architects of Apathy and Their Puffed-Up Pupils:

Let's take a closer look at the severe, whip-cracking side of Jesus. The tender, loving Shepherd suddenly morphs into a stern drill sergeant with unyielding demands.

Picture the scene: A crowd on the edge of their seats, minds reeling as Jesus calmly equates a flicker of anger with murder and a fleeting glance with adultery. The tension in the air thickens like bad soup when He suggests it's better to gouge out an eye or lop off a hand than to face the flames of Hell (Matthew 5:29–30). This isn't exactly the "Good Shepherd" you'd expect on a Hallmark card, is it? But did Jesus change—or is it our understanding that needs a makeover?

Think about it: Jesus wasn't launching a fear campaign or promoting some twisted version of spiritual amputation. No, He was slicing through the fluffy layers of self-righteousness and rule-keeping, pulling back the curtain on the core issue—our desperate need for grace and the utter futility of trying to save ourselves through sweat and sacrifice.

The Sermon on the Mount, through the lens of grace, doesn't come off as a how-to manual for achieving sainthood. It's more like a giant billboard announcing: YOU CAN'T DO THIS—BUT HE CAN. Jesus wasn't setting us up for failure—He was pointing to the cross, where the impossible demands of the Law were not only met but crushed.

So, when Jesus lays it on thick, He's not trying to scare us straight. He's shaking us out of the delusion that we can somehow pull this off on our own. His stern words are like a spiritual intervention—telling us to ditch the flimsy life raft of self-made righteousness and cling to the solid rock of His finished work.

Let's break it down: Is there any reason to fear Jesus? Nah. He's not here to be scary—He's grace personified, inviting us into a relationship built on love, not a never-ending to-do list of moral perfection.

In Christ, we're free to live authentically, with no more paralyzing fear of failure hanging over our heads. Our standing with God doesn't hinge on perfect compliance with impossible rules but on His rock-solid promises to us.

Can we say, "Jesus nailed the whole Law, so I'm off the hook"? You bet. This is not a flippant dismissal of moral responsibility but a bold declaration of the sufficiency of Christ's sacrifice. The Law isn't just fulfilled—it's superseded, leaving us with a whole new way to live, guided by the Spirit, not imprisoned by the letter.

Our new hearts, installed by the Holy Spirit, naturally lean toward love. We don't need to dissect every motive or action like spiritual forensic scientists. Now we can live free—authentic, joyful, and in constant connection with Jesus—because it's no longer about keeping score. It's about resting in His finished work.

In light of this, let's look at the Sermon on the Mount not as a soul-crushing checklist but as a spotlight on our need for grace. Jesus didn't throw down a gauntlet to test our religious stamina. His words invite us to step into a New Covenant where the Law is fulfilled, and our lives are powered by His Spirit, not driven by our own failing efforts.

Here's to ditching the checklist, embracing freedom, and living in the overflow of grace—because the Law's a done deal, and we've got something far better carrying us now.

In grace that frees and fuels,
Andronicus and Johannes

BEYOND STONE

To the Ministers of the Mosaic and Their Thirsty Flocks:

Here we are, your humble scribes, dishing out the delectable freedom served up by Christ. It's a freedom that liberates us from the shackles of the Law. And yes, this includes those Ten Commandments that Moses brought down not as party favors, but as a sobering reminder of our inability to measure up.

Let's cut to the chase: You've been handed a get-out-of-Law-free card that goes far beyond dietary quirks to the very crux of the Ten Commandments. Bold claim? Absolutely. But Paul was not shy about calling the Commandments a "ministry of death" and "a ministry of condemnation" (2 Corinthians 3:7–11). No, this isn't throwing shade at the Law. It's calling it what it is—perfect, yes, but also an impossible taskmaster, a cold-blooded killer pinpointing our spiritual death with surgical precision. And it's about elevating the magnificent grace and freedom found in the Spirit's embrace.

The Apostle Paul hits us with a truth bomb in Romans 7:7–8, spotlighting "You shall not covet" (one of the Big Ten!) as sin's springboard, only to insightfully note that sin's pretty much a dead issue without the Law. Here lies the heart of the matter: the Law's an impressive guidepost, steering us straight to Christ's sufficiency, where sin's power deflates faster than a balloon at a porcupine convention.

But if you wander into almost any church today, you'll stumble into a legalistic quagmire, with folks striving to "get right with God" as if grace was just a starting point. The Law's perfect demands, which only Christ met two thousand years ago, were never meant to be a stairway to heaven—they're more like a neon sign screaming for a Savior.

As new creations, we're not under the old schoolmaster's thumb but are moving freely under grace. Holding on to the Ten Commandments as your moral compass in the Spirit-led life? That's like using an ancient blueprint for a cave-dweller's hut to design a sleek, glass-walled penthouse—completely out of its league.

Even James (you know, the strict one) chips in, reminding us that flunking one law equals bombing them all (James 2:10). This all-in-or-fold approach squashes any dreams of God grading on a curve, highlighting our need for rightness by faith rather than self-righteous box-ticking.

The Law's gig as our divine tutor (Galatians 3:24) was always to chauffeur us to Christ, not chain us to an endless loop of sin and self-condemnation. It spotlighted our flat tires and nudged us toward the One who crossed the finish line for us. In Him, we're not slaves to a bygone system but children of a loving Father.

Clinging to a Law-centric gospel is like missing the forest for the trees, planting seeds in soil better suited for struggle than for thriving in Christ. For where the Spirit of the Lord is, there's liberty

(2 Corinthians 3:17)—freedom from condemnation and empowerment to live vibrantly through the indwelling Jesus.

So, dear Church, it's high time we woke up to our New Covenant reality. The Law, with its detailed do's and don'ts, has been overshadowed by the superior promise of grace. Let's jettison the old way and grab hold of the new.

Leaders, we beseech you: Teach this freedom, preach this freedom, live this freedom—for in doing so, we honor the Law by acknowledging its perfect and impossible standard and its ultimate purpose: to guide us to the endless grace and truth found only in Jesus Christ.

In Paul's electrifying words from Romans 7:4, we're reminded that our death to the Law through Christ enables us to bear fruit for God. This is fruit not cultivated by compliance with the Ten Commandments but by living in and from Jesus. Remember: It's the fruit of the Spirit, not the fruit of the Law.

This fruit is borne not from stone tablets but from the vibrant life of Christ within us, far surpassing anything the Law could hope to cultivate. In embracing Christ without the stone tablets, we discover godliness that springs from Him alone.

So what if Jesus Christ—risen and reigning in your heart—was your only motivation for living right? Now, wouldn't that be something to shout about?

In love and liberty,
Andronicus and Johannes

MISREAD INSCRIPTIONS

To the Legal Eagles of the Lord's House and the Seekers of Light, Lost in Legalism's Labyrinth:

Ah, the enduring saga of the Old Testament Law and its role—or notable lack thereof—in the life of us, the New Covenant crowd. In a twist that would have even Paul doing a double-take, some folks now claim that the very law Christ set us free from is somehow etched onto our hearts.

"Hold up," you might say, "Didn't Hebrews 10:16, with a nod to good old Jeremiah, talk about this laws-etching business upon our hearts?" Sure, some might think we're getting the Old Testament band back together, commandments and all, right in our New Covenant hearts. But wait—plot hole detected!

Paul, ever the pot-stirrer, lays out the truth in Galatians 2:19, "For through the Law I died to the Law so that I might live to God." Dead to the Law, yet some suggest it's alive and kicking in our hearts? And let's not forget Romans 6:14, where Paul insists, "For sin shall not be master over you, for you are not under law but under grace." If we've died to the Law, how can it be making a guest appearance in our hearts?

The plot thickens with that sneaky little plural—“laws”—in Hebrews 10:16. But don’t panic, it’s not about reviving the 613 Old Testament commandments. It’s about something entirely fresh and liberating, brought to life in the New Covenant.

At this point, faith and love, as championed by the Apostle John, enter stage left: “This is His commandment, that we believe in the name of His Son Jesus Christ, and love one another, just as He commanded us” (1 John 3:23). Notice the simplicity? Two commands: believe and love. It’s not a reboot of the Old Testament; it’s a whole new game.

Jesus himself says in John 13:34, “A new commandment I give to you, that you love one another, even as I have loved you, that you also love one another.” This is not an update, not a sequel, but an entirely new commandment, replacing the old way with love that flows from the Spirit, not from sweat and tears.

And here’s the kicker: Loving God with all your heart, soul, and mind and loving your neighbor as yourself? Sure, they’re noble quests. But under the Law, they’re akin to crossing the Sahara Desert barefoot with nothing but a leaky water bottle. Jesus pointed to these as *the greatest commands within the Law* to spotlight our need for something else—Him.

Claiming the Old Testament Law is back in business in our hearts is like suggesting we bring back dial-up internet in the era of fiber-optic Wi-Fi. Who’s signing up for that? Under the New Covenant, it’s not trying our best to love God and others through willpower. Instead, it’s about diving headfirst into the ocean of God’s love, letting the currents of His affection sweep us into loving others—not out of duty, but as a natural overflow of the love we've soaked in.

Dear saints, let's not hitch our wagons to a confusing mashup of old and new covenants. The Old Testament Law did its job, leading us to Christ where real freedom awaits (Galatians 3:24–25). Now, under grace, we're invited to a way of faith and love, etched not on stone but on hearts transformed by the Spirit.

So, it's not about cranking up your Love-O-Meter for God and neighbor, Old Testament style. It's about basking in how much He loves us and letting that love fuel everything. Then it's the work of the Spirit, as natural to us as breathing.

In His profound love,
Andronicus and Johannes

UNSHACKLED GENEROSITY

To the Tax Collectors of Today and the Trustees of the Tithe:

In this delightful era where the lines between tradition and transformation blur more than your vision after a long day deciphering the fine print of Leviticus, we find ourselves at a fascinating crossroads. It seems like the age-old practice of tithing is strutting around, dressed up in the ill-fitting costumes of religious obligation.

Ah, tithing! That sacred ten percent, pitched as a non-negotiable ticket to God's favor, or so the sales pitch goes. Have we not drifted into a legalistic lagoon, swapping the boundless skies of grace for the cramped cubicle of obligation? This dear tradition, rooted deeply in the soils of the Law, seems to have sprouted thorns that prick at the very heart of the Gospel's freedom.

Let's peel back the layers, shall we? The push, nudge, and sometimes shove towards securing tithes from the congregation often reveals a misunderstanding so profound it would make the Apostle Paul cringe in dismay. God, the infinite Creator, isn't digging through our wallets for loose change—He's inviting us to discover the boundless riches found in Christ. The Apostle Paul championed a model of giving that sings of voluntary support—no guilt trips, no flashy theatrics (2 Corinthians 9:5). Contrast this with the flashy, arm-twisting escapades some modern churches embark on, turning giving into a performance rather than an act of heartfelt worship.

Digging into the archives, we find that tithing was just another part of the Old Covenant's time-stamped blueprint. However, let's not forget that we Gentiles were never under those ancient commandments. Christ's ultimate sacrifice heralded a new era—an era of grace, not of adherence to ancient statutes. Dragging Old Testament verses into modern tithing debates like hired guns not only muddies our freedom in Christ but warps giving into a transaction, not a testament of gratitude (Galatians 3:24–25).

Enter Abraham and Melchizedek in their Hebrews 7 cameo—where Abraham's one-off gift gets miscast as a standing order for church coffers. This singular act of respect, far removed from our Sunday offerings, can be explained in a greater-than sketch:

Melchizedek > Abraham
Jesus > Levi (in Abraham's lineage)
New Covenant > Old Covenant

Simple, huh? That's the real Hebrews 7 takeaway. It was about comparing priests and covenants. And priest Jesus (in the order of Melchizedek) and His new covenant come out on top. That's all there is to it. Not once does the author of Hebrews say it's about us swiping our credit cards.

And then there's the prosperity gospel, that alluring song that promises rain showers of riches in return for your tithes. Friends, this is a gross distortion of the Gospel, reducing God's grace to a cosmic vending machine—insert tithes, receive blessings. God isn't some mafia kingpin you pay off to keep the universe running smoothly.

Furthermore, Jesus's critique of the Pharisees in Matthew 23:23 wasn't an encore for tithing but a spotlight on their hypocrisy as they forked over their tithe well enough but neglected the weightier matters of the Law. (By the way, did you notice this proves that tithing is a "matter of the Law"? And hey, you're not under the Law.)

Our gatherings, dear family, are not tax collection venues but celebrations of grace, community, and a shared message. The New Testament paints giving as a liberating, life-giving act, springing from hearts transformed by Christ's love.

Interestingly, statistics show that today's churchgoers aren't even hitting the 10 percent mark. This starkly illustrates that the contemporary tithing teaching is not achieving its intended goal. This beckons us to a grace-filled model of giving, where amounts are not dictated by percentages but by the joy and willingness of the giver's heart (2 Corinthians 9:7).

As we stand at this crossroads, let's choose the path illuminated by the liberating power of the Gospel. May our giving break free from the chains of guilt and compulsion. Let's give, not because we're trapped by tradition, but because we're carried by the current of grace. After all, we're not chasing blessings or dodging curses—we're simply responding to the boundless love already ours.

Let's give, not out of duty but from delight, embracing the privilege of partnering with God in His transforming work. And let's never forget: the grace of God doesn't pause when we reach for our wallets.

In the love of our liberating Lord,
Andronicus and Johannes

TRUE SPIRITUAL REPOSE

To the Silent Sufferers in the Seats:

Let's have a little heart-to-heart, shall we, about the Sabbath and the exquisite art of resting in the finished work of Christ—an art as lost to the modern church as the concept of patience in rush-hour traffic (you know, that rare virtue we reserve for Netflix buffering).

Reflect, if you will, on Hebrews 4:9–10: "So there remains a Sabbath rest for the people of God. For the one who has entered His rest has himself also rested from his works, as God did from His." Here, it's not about a day to be ticked off but a Person to be embraced. Forget the checklists; it's about collapsing into grace.

Remember how it all went down. God wrapped up creation in six days and took a leisure day not because He needed a break, but to admire His flawless craftsmanship because, let's face it, who wouldn't admire that masterpiece? And we were made on Day 6 and invited not as contributors but as partakers of this perfection.

Fast forward to the mirror image in the New Testament. We see the finished work of Christ—His crucifixion, burial, and resurrection—and they were executed flawlessly without our help, as if we could ever improve on perfection. Then we were handed the backstage pass to the ultimate masterpiece. The striking parallel here is as intentional as it is beautiful—just as humanity was invited to rest in God's completed creation, we are beckoned to rest in the completed work of Christ.

This rest is not a call to passivity but a cease-fire of our spiritual striving under the Law, a white surrender flag in the war of self-righteousness. With our rap sheet cleared, our guilt removed, and our standing before God secured, the Law's relentless grind has been fulfilled in Christ. We step into a new era—a covenant of grace, where our relationship with God is anchored in the finished work of Christ.

In Him, we find a new identity, a fresh start, not because we embarked on a self-improvement spree but because we are made new in Christ—complete, accepted, and thoroughly loved. This is the real Sabbath rest—a halt in our hamster-wheel hustle to curry favor with God, a favor we already bask in, thanks to Christ.

The Sabbath, in the Old Testament, was the trailer to the blockbuster that is Christ. Under the New Covenant, we're not hitched to any command to observe the Sabbath day. White-knuckling the Sabbath like a life raft is like preferring the trailer over the movie. Who needs spoilers when you've got the real thing?

The spiritual rest we have in Christ transcends a day—it's a 24/7, 365-day kind of rest that infiltrates every aspect of our lives. But in a culture obsessed with spiritual boot camps that promise to make us "radical" for God, we've somehow turned Christianity into an extreme sport. "Step out of your comfort zone," they say. "Give till it hurts." And let's not forget the spiritual regimens that make Pilates look like child's play. Hey, if the idea of a "Bible-based diet" doesn't make you pause, we don't know what will. Who knew grace came with carb-counting?

This relentless push towards doing, towards crafting a spirituality of our own making, is nothing short of exhausting. It's a carnival of contradiction, where the message seems to be "You're not under the law, but here's how you should follow it anyway." We're already forgiven, yet we're asked to seek forgiveness from God daily. We're right with God, yet constantly urged to get right with God. It's a spiritual hall of mirrors, leaving us disoriented and far from rested.

The simplicity of the Gospel has been buried under a mountain of spiritual to-do lists, leaving us wheezing for grace. The last thing we need is a fixation with a Friday-Saturday religious observance, clocking in for divine roll call. So here's to resting, really resting, in the finished work of Christ.

In a delightful twist of irony, we're saying: Let's "get busy" resting in God's grace, shall we? Because let's face it, burnout isn't a spiritual gift.

Here's to relaxation in Jesus,
Andronicus and Johannes

PART 2

EMBRACE GRACE!

THE "WORK" IS TO BELIEVE

To the Districts of Dogma and Their Drowning Disciples:

How we adore our spiritual treadmills, don't we? Racing to outdo each other in a marathon of holiness, yet somehow always ending up panting at the starting line. "Do I have enough works to show for my faith? Am I really saved?" you ask, while nervously glancing at your spiritual Fitbit. Relax, breathe, and let's continue our journey through the cobwebbed corners of legalism you've grown so fond of.

Let's dive into the meat of the matter, shall we? James throws a wrench in our comfy theological chairs by daring to suggest we are "justified by works" not once, not twice, but thrice!

- "Was not Abraham our father justified by works . . . ?" (James 2:21)
- "A man is justified by works and not by faith alone" (James 2:24)
- "Was not Rahab the harlot also justified by works . . . ?" (James 2:25)

Martin Luther nearly had a theological meltdown over this, deeming James less suited for Scripture than a cat in a dog show. It's enough to make even a Reformer sweat. Yet, here we are, grappling with the same old conundrum. The Greek word for "justify" plays no favorites between James 2:24 and Romans 3:28, showing up to the party dressed the same way in both verses. Imagine that.

Now, before you start stockpiling good deeds like a doomsday prepper, let's pause. James isn't calling us to become spiritual hoarders. The passage says Abraham, our forefather of faith, was justified when he decided to play "Extreme Makeover: Altar Edition" with Isaac—once. Rahab, an unexpected hero, swung her door open for the spies—once. These were not recurring events, but singular responses borne of faith.

This so-called justification by works that James harps about? It's about a one-time response to God's nudge, not a lifetime subscription to "Good Deeds Monthly." If you've ever swung open the door of your heart to Jesus, like Rahab did for those spies, congratulations! If you've ever offered yourself to Jesus like Abe offered Isaac, again, congratulations! You've responded to the Gospel, and you've checked the James 2 box. No need to keep a tally or lose sleep over whether you've "done enough" in life. James isn't the spiritual auditor we've made him out to be.

So, let's not lose our marbles over this, shall we? Everyone trips and falls (take a breath and read James 3:2 sometime). If stumbling were a deal-breaker, we'd all be out of the running. Remember, "if we are faithless, He remains faithful" (2 Timothy 2:13). God isn't your hall monitor standing by with a clipboard, marking our every misstep. He's in it for the long haul, no matter how many spiritual faceplants we do.

As for daily acts of kindness and love? They're not your ticket to salvation but rather the natural outflow of a life intertwined with Jesus. Like walking into a room God has already lit up for us, ready for us to explore and enjoy. There's no need to bring your own lightbulb.

In short, it's time to hang up our Pharisaical robes and dance in the freedom Christ has gifted us. You've already responded to the ultimate altar call. Now, live like it, laugh a little, and for heaven's sake, enjoy Jesus.

Smiling because the work is to believe (John 6:29),
Andronicus and Johannes

HOLDING OR HELD?

To the Gatekeepers of Gracelessness:

The halls of contemporary religious chatter echo with the sound of cluelessness! At the forefront of these distorted melodies is the confusion surrounding the phrase "fallen from grace" from Galatians. Many have turned this into a full-blown tragic opera, mistaking it for a sob story about Christians supposedly losing their salvation. Let's be clear: this interpretation is nothing more than creative fiction.

Paul, in his letter to the Galatians, wasn't penning a suspense thriller about believers losing their salvation. Rather, he was addressing those high on their own supply of legalism, believing they could earn their way into God's favor. "You have been severed from Christ, you who are seeking to be justified by law; you have fallen from grace," Paul warns in Galatians 5:4, not as a somber goodbye to the saved but as a wake-up call to those who were betting on the wrong horse—their own sweaty efforts instead of Christ's finished work.

Jesus Himself declared that the life He gives is eternal and irreversible (Luke 20:36), assuring us that no one can pry us out of His grip (John 10:28–29). The New Testament doesn't flirt with the idea of eternal security—it marries it. Jesus, our divine assurance agent, locks it in with an unbreakable bond. John backs Him up, confirming that believers already possess eternal life (1 John 5:13)—and note, it's eternal life, not some trial subscription. Paul closes the case by saying the Holy Spirit is our down payment (Ephesians 1:13–14), locking in God's gifts and calling, which are as irrevocable as His love (Romans 11:29, 8:38–39). The writer of Hebrews paints a picture of our hope as unshakable and anchored in the granite-solid promises of God (Hebrews 6:17–19). This hope, moored to the very character of God, is sure and steady, resting not on our performance (which fluctuates like the stock market) but on our God's unwavering faithfulness.

And what about Matthew 7:23, where Jesus utters the chilling statement, "I never knew you"? Well, let's not twist this into a cruel tale of believers getting dissed by Christ. This is about those who mistook spiritual résumé-building for genuine faith. It's not about genuine believers getting the cold shoulder from our Savior. These folks were so focused on their spiritual LinkedIn profiles that they missed the heart of the Gospel—salvation by grace through faith, not by showcasing a spiritual highlight reel.

Our tour of assurance takes a scenic route through Revelation, where the fear of being "blotted out" of the Book of Life gets debunked. Revelation 3:5 isn't God holding a divine eraser over us, ready to wipe us out; it's the opposite—a rock-solid guarantee that our names will *never* be removed from God's ledger. And that whole "lukewarm" fiasco in Revelation 3:16? That's a divine nudge for purposeful living, not a salvation temperature check. It's not about being "on fire" for the Lord. It's more like, "Be hot, be cold, be something."

Even the rallying cries to "continue" and "hold fast" (Colossians 1:23; 1 Corinthians 15:2) are not spiritual scare tactics. They're Paul's motivational pep talks for those teetering on the fence, urging them to get off the sidelines and fully embrace the Gospel they've heard. It's an evangelistic elbow in the ribs, not a salvation yank.

So, let's bid adieu to the melodrama of losing salvation and dive headfirst into the joy-filled liberation of God's grace. Our relationship with God isn't a shaky round of spiritual Jenga. It's set on the immovable foundation of God's faithfulness, not our wobbly human attempts. In short, if your salvation depended on you, you'd be in trouble. But good news—it doesn't. It depends on the One who doesn't change, doesn't fail, and doesn't break a promise.

Celebrating the enduring security we have in Christ,
Andronicus and Johannes

SALVATION SCAM

To the Battered Believers and the Wandering Worshipers:

We pen this letter to expose a particularly pernicious piece of piffle that's been parading through the hallowed halls of Christendom: the so-called Lordship Salvation. It's time to expose this theological trainwreck for what it is—an exhausting and deceptive doctrine that muddles the Gospel and leaves believers in a constant state of spiritual anxiety. Let's peel back the layers of this mess, shall we?

First off, let's settle this once and for all: Jesus is Lord. Always has been, always will be. When you called upon Him for salvation, you acknowledged His Lordship implicitly. There's no separate, magical moment where you need to "make" Him Lord. It's like saying you need to make the sun shine or water wet. Laughable, right? He is Lord by virtue of who He is, not by virtue of our recognition.

Some of you have been battered by the message that you need to do more, be more, and strive harder to prove your salvation. You've been told that God is only in love with a future, better version of you. You've heard it a thousand times: more quiet times, more volunteering, more witnessing, more proving—just more of everything. It's as if God's affection is a carrot on a stick, always just out of reach. But here's the kicker: God loves you right now, as you are, not as you "could be" someday. You are a fragrant aroma to Him (2 Corinthians 2:15). You smell great to the Almighty!

The problem with Lordship Salvation is it conflates justification with sanctification, mixing up our new birth in Christ with our performance. Ephesians 2:8–9 doesn't mince words: "For it is by grace you have been saved, through faith—and this is not from yourselves, it is the gift of God—not by works, so that no one can boast." Salvation is a gift, folks. It's not a loan you have to repay with good behavior.

Why do we insist on turning a wide-open invitation into an obstacle course to get to Jesus? And once someone accepts Him, why make salvation feel like a slippery prize they have to keep from dropping? They were counting on what Jesus did to be enough. But then we bring in "Lordship Salvation." This isn't your garden-variety salvation, mind you. This is Lordship Salvation. More self-dependent, more grievous and oh, so much less certain. Have you noticed that we tend to do this in almost every aspect of this entire faith? It seems we are not content until we make salvation at least somewhat dependent upon man's ability.

Let's talk about the absurdity of trying to "keep" Jesus as Lord. If you buy into this, then every slip-up leaves you questioning whether He's still Lord over your life. How do you get Him back? Twelve more Bible studies? Three more church services? Witness to six more people? Recite "I submit" like it's a magic spell? No, this notion is a fraud. Jesus is Lord by His nature, and your faith in Him recognizes that.

Lordship Salvation often leads to a focus on external behavior rather than internal faith, creating a legalistic mindset. This misplaced emphasis on performance over grace turns the Gospel into a burdensome checklist rather than a liberating truth. And oh, the legalism! The idea that you must produce a laundry list of good works to prove your salvation is nothing short of spiritual slavery.

You know He is Lord, right? He doesn't need you to make Him so. The thief on the cross is so grateful he didn't have to go through your new stipulations. Life is tough enough as it is. We've got the world, the flesh, the power of sin, and telemarketers to deal with already. Why do you insist on making His easy yoke into a never-ending defense and proof of their worthiness? Does that not sound at least a little bit strange to you?

Now, to the heart of the matter: Lordship Salvation undermines the assurance of salvation, and 1 John 5:13 gives us confidence: "I write these things to you who believe in the name of the Son of God so that you may know that you have eternal life." Assurance comes from trusting in Christ's perfect work, not in our imperfect efforts.

So why are we acting like we need to finish what He started? It's either finished or it's not. There's no middle ground here. Either Jesus nailed it, or He didn't. It's time we embrace the truth that sets us free and ditch the exhausting, fraudulent notion that we need to add to Christ's finished work.

The Gospel is stunningly simple: Jesus did it all. Flawlessly. No do-overs necessary. When He cried, "It is finished," He meant it.

Confident in the perfect, completed work of our Lord Jesus Christ,
Andronicus and Johannes

ANCHOR OF ASSURANCE

To the High Council of Holy Critiques and Their Caged Creatures:

The modern church appears to be adrift in a sea of tradition, tossed by the fickle winds of change, all while blindfolded to the dazzling brilliance of the Gospel's simplicity.

As a result, Hebrews 6 and 10 have been warped into weapons of mass confusion instead of the beacons of hope they were meant to be. Some have twisted these passages with their talk of "falling away" and "no sacrifice left," into a narrative so bleak it could make a sunny day feel like a midnight walk through a graveyard.

Let's set the record straight: Hebrews was penned for those caught in the awkward dance between two covenants—the Old, with its penchant for rituals and sacrifices, and the New, which essentially says, "Been there, done that, got the t-shirt thanks to Jesus." It's not a tale of woe for believers who've somehow lost their grip on salvation but a stern talking-to for those who treat the Gospel like a wine tasting—swishing it around, nodding appreciatively, but never actually swallowing.

When Hebrews 6 wags its finger about "falling away," it's not lamenting over those who are snug in Christ's embrace suddenly doing a backflip into damnation. No, it's about folks who've sampled heaven's truth and somehow still prefer the tasteless idea of their current lives. It's akin to choosing a stale cracker over a feast because you fancy the wrapper.

This is exactly why we see words like "enlightened" and "tasted" and why the author references "ground that drinks in the rain" versus ground that doesn't. Then, just to clear up any lingering confusion, he reassures the true believers with the promise of beautiful things that "accompany their salvation." It's almost as if he's waving a sign that says, "Don't worry, I'm not talking about you." He's all too aware that some might misinterpret his words, and he wants to make sure they don't lose sleep over it.

And Hebrews 10? Please, that's not about losing your salvation like you misplace your car keys. It's about the colossal blunder of seeing grace, personified in Christ, and saying, "Thanks, but no thanks." This isn't about tripping over your own feet; it's about willfully sprinting in the opposite direction of salvation.

Diving deeper, the Old Covenant is likened to a shadow—because, let's be honest, who in their right mind chooses a shadow over the real thing? This is about swapping the temporary for the eternal, about missing the forest for the trees. Those "falling away" aren't losing salvation; they're just stubbornly refusing to receive it in the first place.

The warnings in Hebrews 6 and 10 are not spiritual nightmares designed to keep believers up at night. They're urgent shout-outs to the fence-sitters, begging them not to tumble back into the abyss of unbelief but to step boldly into God's grace, once and for all.

This new life is about assurance, not anxiety; it's about the rock-solid guarantee of salvation for everyone in Christ. And to those who misinterpret these texts as a narrative of insecurity and fear, let's be clear: You're not just missing the boat—you're paddling furiously in the wrong direction.

Look, the Gospel isn't a horror story where salvation is dangled like a carrot on a stick, always just out of reach. It's the ultimate love story where the ending is so gloriously assured that it should make us leap for joy, not shiver in fear.

We're not called to live on a diet of spiritual antacids, terrified of losing our salvation at the next hiccup. We're invited to feast on the certainty of our redemption, secure in the knowledge that our place at God's table is reserved forever.

So, let's reclaim the narrative here:

> For if we go on sinning willfully after receiving the knowledge of the truth, there no longer remains a sacrifice for sins. (Hebrews 10:26)

Hebrews 10's warning about "if we go on sinning willfully" is not about sharing someone else's Netflix subscription. No, the only kind of sin mentioned for ten straight chapters in Hebrews is the sin of *unbelief*. So, it's not a tale of woe for the underperforming believer but a stark reminder for the fence-sitter of what's at stake. If anyone rejects the truth of the cross, there's simply no other sacrifice out there that will do the job.

Brothers and sisters, the grace you've been handed in Christ isn't some fragile trinket ready to shatter. It's as enduring as the promise of God Himself. For those who've embraced this truth, rest easy. Your salvation isn't a candle flickering in the wind but a fire blazing brightly—a testament to the unshakable love and faithfulness of our Savior. So, let's rest in His finished work and stop treating salvation like a limited-time offer—because it's more solid than any deal you'll ever find.

In the unyielding grip of His grace,
Andronicus and Johannes

DON'T BE SCARED

To the Holy Heralds of Hypocrisy and Their Fearful Followers:

Let's unpack the absurdity of living in constant fear of a God who, ironically, went out of His way to declare, "Fear not." It's as if the divine memo, scrawled in heavenly ink, got lost somewhere between the pearly gates and our inbox.

Let's start with the basics: Jesus picked up our tab. Yes, the whole thing. "For the wages of sin is death, but the free gift of God is eternal life in Christ Jesus our Lord" (Romans 6:23). Picture Christ on the cross, receipt in hand, securely saying, "I've got this one." Yet, here we are, fretting over a bill that's already been settled. Past, present, future sins? Taken away. Let that sink in before you start hyperventilating over your spiritual debt repayment.

Now, on to this whole "fear and trembling" business from Philippians 2:12. Some seem to have taken this as a divine directive to quake in their boots every time they think of God. A closer look (perhaps take a screenshot and zoom in) reveals Paul is talking about a reverential awe, not a fright fest. This is about the kind of respect that has us marveling at God's majesty, not hiding under the bed:

> work out your salvation with fear and trembling; for it is God who is at work in you, both to will and to work for His good pleasure. (Philippians 2:12b–13)

Verse 13 gently reminds us that it's God doing the heavy lifting within us. This is comforting, not alarming. The journey is about growing in grace, shepherded by the Spirit. Picture God as the Sculptor, and we're the clay—except the clay's having a full-blown panic attack, convinced it has to shape itself.

"Perfect love casts out fear" (1 John 4:18). This gem of wisdom shows us that the more we marinate in God's love, the less we should be shaking in our sandals. Our relationship with God is rooted in His epic love story, sending His Son to save us. It's hard to square that with the idea that He's also lurking in the shadows, waiting to smite us for every slip-up.

And for those who still cling to the notion that God's ideal relationship dynamic involves our being scared stiff, let's mull over this: God's in the business of wiping away tears (Revelation 21:4), not collecting them. When Jesus walked on water and it spooked His disciples, His next move wasn't to say "Boo!" but rather, "Take courage! It is I. Do not be afraid." Clearly, God is not aiming for a Fear Factor vibe in our relationship with Him.

Yet, the Bible does endorse a healthy dose of fear—fear as in respect, awe, the kind that makes you go "Wow, God is awesome" and not "Wow, I need a bigger blanket to hide under." This kind of fear is the starter kit for wisdom (Proverbs 9:10) and serves as a reality check, reminding us to fear (respect) God.

Even "fear and trembling" is about appreciating the miracle of "Christ in you" with the seriousness it deserves—think reverence, not terror. After all, the God who flung stars into space and keeps the universe ticking calls us His children (see Romans 8:15; Galatians 4:6). That's an awe-inspiring love that should leave us all just a little breathless.

We can retire the old "fear of God" image and embrace a relationship with God marked by love, reverence, and awe. After all, if God wanted us terrified, He probably wouldn't have gone to such lengths to show us His love that's literally out of this world. So, let's trade in our trembling for trust, and stop treating God like a cosmic taskmaster when He's been the Savior all along.

Filled with godly excitement (and not afraid),
Andronicus and Johannes

SIN'S ANTIDOTE

To Grace's Gravediggers:

In your quest for holiness, you've ironically clung to a lifeless shell of religiosity, mistaking the husk for the heart of it. Oh, how you've twisted the beautiful, liberating concept of grace into something unrecognizable!

Romans 6:14 has been clear: "For sin shall not be master over you, for you are not under law but under grace." Yet, here we are, listening to your cries of "greasy grace," "cheap grace," and "hyper-grace." Your fear that grace might unleash some tidal wave of sin is as laughable as it is tragic.

Let's get one thing straight: God's grace isn't a divine loophole to exploit but a power-packed promise of transformation. The very suggestion that grace could ever be a green light for sinning is absurd to anyone who's actually tasted its life-changing power. And yet, in your zeal to guard against an imaginary license to sin, you've missed the point entirely. (Note: You do seem to be sinning just fine without a license.)

Your favorite identity crisis—insisting we're "dirty, rotten sinners" even after being born of the Spirit—is a masterclass in completely missing the mark. It's a wonder you don't trip over your own contradictions, preaching freedom in Christ one moment and then chaining yourselves to sin the next. If only you could see that acknowledging our identity as new-hearted saints is the first step toward actual godliness, not a plunge into depravity.

And then there's your bizarre fear of "too much grace," as if such a thing exists. It's as though you think the Almighty somehow overshot with a clumsy miscalculation. "Oops, too much grace! They might start believing they're loved and forgiven. Can't have that!" This fear reveals someone who is tragically unfamiliar with the nature of God's grace, which is the very thing that empowers us to live lives that reflect Him.

Your call for a "balance" between grace and law as if they were ingredients in a recipe exposes a woeful ignorance of their respective roles. The law, as Paul pointed out, was never about achieving righteousness but about exposing our need for grace. Saying we need a bit of both is like claiming you need a dash of poison to really enjoy the meal.

In your misguided attempts to protect the church from the so-called dangers of grace, you've erected barriers where there should be bridges, promoting a gospel of self-effort that Paul would have vehemently opposed. Your mantra seems to be "Grace got us in, but our hustle keeps us hanging on."

So, here's a novel idea: Instead of fearing grace, dive into its depths. And while you're at it, ditch the self-help sermons and preach Christ crucified and risen. Embrace the freedom of being fully loved, fully forgiven, and fully equipped by grace to live from God's Spirit.

Get back to the heart of the Gospel. Only then will you grasp the inspiration of God's grace and the transformation it brings.

In His outrageous empowerment,
Andronicus and Johannes, trying to make sense of your fascination with chains.

PREDESTINATION PUZZLE

To the Chasers of Conformity and the Lost Lambs in the Land of Legalism:

Congratulations! You've transformed the joyous news of the Gospel into something as palatable as stale bread. You've managed to take the profound doctrine of predestination and turn it into a theological cage match between Team Calvin and Team Arminius, missing the point entirely. Bravo!

Now, let's pause this pathetic parade of exclusivity to revisit the shockingly inclusive nature of the Gospel, as outlined by none other than the Apostle Paul—yes, that tent-making, prison-frequenting maverick who had the nerve to suggest that God's grace just might be for, wait for it, everyone. Predestination, as Paul saw it, isn't God playing "eeny, meeny, miny, moe" with humanity. Nope, this is about an all-access pass for anyone—Jews, Gentiles, left-handed people, even those who can't whistle.

It's like realizing that your exclusive country club just opened its doors to the public, and guess what? Not everyone's thrilled. Ever wondered why Paul drones on for chapters in Romans and Ephesians about predestination and God's "right to choose"? This is why: He's defending God's right to save "those dirty, rotten Gentiles," and in doing so, he's defending his job as an apostle to them.

So, before you whip out Jacob, Esau, or Pharaoh's hardened heart as your ace in the hole, remember: Paul's not running a fantasy salvation league. These stories highlight God's sovereignty to pick whoever He wants and—spoiler alert: He's picking the Gentiles (not just the Jews). So, this was never about random individuals winning a salvation lottery. After all, Jesus mentions drawing *everyone* to Himself in John 12:32. That's not a throwaway tweet; it's the mission statement of the cross. The cross is God's magnet, attracting a diverse crowd from across the globe.

Romans 9:30 crashes the elitist party, suggesting that those heathen Gentiles—who weren't even trying to score points with God—got in on the righteousness-by-faith deal.

> What shall we say then? That Gentiles, who did not pursue righteousness, attained righteousness, even the righteousness which is by faith. . . . (Romans 9:30)

That right there is proof that God's invite list is way broader than we'd like to admit. Apparently, God's master plan features a surprise guest appearance by the Gentiles.

Ephesians digs even deeper into this, showcasing a linguistic ping-pong match between "us/we" (Jews) and "you" (Gentiles):

- He chose us (1:4)
- He predestined us (1:5)

- we, who were the first to put our hope in Christ (1:12)
- and you also were included (1:13)
- formerly you who are Gentiles by birth (2:11)
- you were separate . . . far away (2:12–13)
- [God] made the two groups one (2:14)
- to reconcile both of them (2:16)
- peace to you who were far away (2:17a)
- and peace to those who were near (2:17b)
- through Him we both have access to the Father (2:18)

Did you catch all the you's and the we's? See, this isn't a heavenly case of individual favoritism. It's a revelation of God's game plan to unite all nationalities under the banner of grace. Yes, the true meaning of predestination relates to God's secret plan (now revealed) to include the Gentiles (not just the Jews) in His Gospel invitation.

Our job isn't to gatekeep the kingdom but to roll out the welcome mat, echoing Romans 10:13: "everyone who calls on the name of the Lord will be saved." This isn't about flexing our theological muscles; it's about reflecting God's indiscriminate grace—because remember: He plays no favorites.

As we sit in our pews, sipping the vintage wine of age-old doctrines, let's not get drunk on our own misconceptions. Instead, let's raise a glass to the Gospel's scandalous inclusivity. Let's shelf the sanctimonious sermonizing and embrace our identity as God's diverse family—lefthanders and all.

United by Christ,
Andronicus and Johannes

THE LORD'S LOTTERY?

To the Godly Gamblers Betting on God's Selection:

How do we ask this gently? Are you turning the house of God into a celestial lottery booth? Look, the Big Guy upstairs isn't doling out salvation like a divine raffle at the county fair: "Step right up! Will you score the golden ticket to glory or the consolation prize to oblivion?"

What a spectacle of divine drama you've cooked up.

Imagine, if you will, *Predestination: The Reality Show*. "This season on *Survivor: Heaven's Gates*: Who will survive the salvation showdown? Will it be Team Elect or Team Reject? Stay tuned as God's mysterious choices unfold!" Sounds absurd, right? Yet, that's exactly the soap opera you've scripted, with God in the role of Holy Game Show Host.

Now, before you dust off your copy of Romans and Ephesians, ready to duel at dawn with verses at ten paces, let's take one more stroll down the lesser-traveled path of predestination, shall we? A path strewn with the confetti of misconceptions and the occasional tumbleweed of bad exegesis.

But hark! What light through yonder Scripture breaks? It is the east, and John is the sun, piercing through the fog of our theological theatrics with an announcement so shocking that it could only be divine. "For God so loved the world," he declares, not "For God so loved a select few who happened to crack the heavenly code."

Paul, that renegade apostle to the Gentiles, didn't pen his epistles to promote a spiritual elite but to proclaim a group hug of heavenly proportions. "You're all invited," he bellows across the ages, "Jews, Gentiles, and even those poor souls who pour the milk before the cereal."

The true controversy over predestination isn't about election exclusivity but about the jaw-dropping inclusivity of God's call—a plot twist the Jews never saw coming. So, as you navigate the theological thickets and doctrinal ditches of predestination, remember: It's not about finding out if you're one of the lucky lottery winners. It's about embracing the truth that the lottery was rigged from the start—rigged in favor of grace, rigged for inclusion of Gentiles, rigged so that everyone has the chance to hear the call and respond.

And to those still clutching their theological scratch-offs, hoping for the Almighty's nod: relax. The drawing's done, the winners announced, and newsflash—you're all winners. Welcome to the party. The door's wide open, the table is set, and the only admission ticket you need is the one that's been offered freely to all: an invitation to forgiveness, freedom, and new life in Jesus—on the house.

So, let's toast to God's love so vast, so absurdly all-encompassing, it obliterates our attempts to shrink-wrap it and sell it in the religious marketplace. And just when we thought it couldn't get any better, spare a thought for Uncle Chet, chain-smoking on the porch and still scratching his head over the divine selection process. Guess what, Chet? There's room at the table for you too.

Andronicus and Johannes, the artists formerly known as Calvin's Club

RSVP REQUIRED

To the Blissfully Naïve and the Eternally Secure:

It's high time we addressed this fanciful notion that everyone, no matter what they believe, is riding the celestial escalator to glory. Whether it's full-blown universalism or the sugar-coated "everyone gets a trophy" gospel, it's nothing more than a spiritual fairy tale. Let's pop this balloon with the sharp needle of Scripture, shall we?

When the Apostle John announced that Jesus is the "propitiation for our sins; and not for ours only, but also for those of the whole world" (1 John 2:2), he wasn't handing out universal "get-out-of-hell-free" cards. He was celebrating that Gentiles, not just Jews, are invited to the salvation banquet. This wasn't a blanket endorsement of universal salvation but rather a jubilant proclamation that the invitation list just got bigger, not the gate wider.

And what about Paul's declaration that "God was in Christ reconciling the world to Himself, not counting their trespasses against them" (2 Corinthians 5:19)? Sounds like a universalist's dream, right? But Paul follows up with, "We beg you on behalf of Christ, be reconciled to God" (verse 20). Last we checked, begging suggests urgency—and, more importantly, that a response is required. Reconciliation is a two-way street. Yes, God's made His move. But now it's our turn to RSVP to the Gospel.

Jesus Himself didn't sugarcoat it: "Whoever believes in the Son has eternal life, but whoever rejects the Son will not see life, for God's wrath remains on them" (John 3:36). Pretty straightforward, don't you think? No belief, no life. No RSVP, no salvation.

Jesus spoke of two paths: one narrow and leading to life, the other wide and leading to destruction (Matthew 7:13–14). If everyone is on the same bus to heaven, why even bother mentioning a road to destruction? And remember when the Roman jailer asked, "Sirs, what must I do to be saved?" Paul didn't respond with, "Relax my friend. Everybody gets in. I'm just out here risking my neck in Asia Minor, because I think people might be happier hearing about Jesus." No, he said, "Believe in the Lord Jesus, and you will be *saved*. . . ." (Acts 16:31). Paul knew eternal destinies were at stake.

Jesus' parable of the sheep and the goats (Matthew 25:31–46) is another stark reminder. He didn't say, "Everyone's a sheep now, congrats!" No, He laid out a final reckoning, where faith is the dividing line, culminating in "eternal punishment" for the goats and "eternal life" for the sheep. If universal salvation were true, this parable would be as pointless as sunscreen at midnight.

The New Testament is packed with warnings about the consequences of unbelief. Paul describes deceitful people whose end is according to their deeds (2 Corinthians 11:13–15). Peter warns that God keeps the unrighteous under punishment for the day of judgment (2 Peter 2:4–10). Revelation paints a vivid picture of the final judgment, where anyone not found in the Book of Life is cast into the lake of fire (Revelation 20:12–15). Sobering stuff, right?

Peter adds his voice in Acts 3:19, calling for repentance: "Repent, then, and turn to God, so that your sins may be wiped out." If sins are automatically wiped out, why the call for repentance? The implication is clear: Without repentance (changing your mind about who Jesus is and believing upon Him), there simply is no forgiveness, no matter how rosy our theology.

We can debate all day long that some haven't had a chance to hear the Gospel, and if God is fair, He must find a loophole. Or we could rest in the character of the One who is good beyond our comprehension and loves more fiercely than we ever could. Maybe we should trust His word and leave the unknown to Him. That's a lot better than handing out hall passes written in disappearing ink.

Universal salvation might be a comforting bedtime story, but it's not the Gospel truth. So, the stakes couldn't be higher, and the message couldn't be clearer. Let's tell the world what Jesus did for them and beg them to RSVP before it's too late.

In the unchanging truth and love of Christ,
Andronicus and Johannes

PART 3

THE ART OF ETERNAL AMNESTY

PARDON ME

To the Shepherds Shunning Sheep and Followers of the Flock:

It's high time we had another little heart-to-heart. Amidst today's theological slap-fights and ecclesiastical runway shows, it seems a singular, transformative truth has been relegated to the back pew: the mind-blowing, convention-shattering doctrine of total forgiveness.

Yes, you heard it right. *Total* forgiveness. Past mess-ups? Scrubbed. Present fumbles? Erased. Future faux pas? Pre-canceled. This isn't your grandma's "say three Hail Marys and try to sin a little less" kind of deal. We're talking about a one-stop, sin-removal shop that leaves us whiter than a bleach commercial—courtesy of Jesus's crucifixion. And yet, this cornerstone of Christianity 101 seems to be collecting dust in the doctrinal attic, right next to your enthusiasm for evangelism and that casserole dish you swiped from the church potluck. (Yes, you're forgiven for that too.)

Now, before you clutch your pearls and accuse us again of peddling "cheap grace," let's take a page out of Paul's playbook from Romans 6:1–2:

> What shall we say then? Are we to continue in sin so that grace may increase? May it never be! How shall we who died to sin still live in it?

Paul preemptively nukes the idea that grace is a golden ticket to the Sin Olympics. Grace, instead of being a license to sin, is the very dynamite that blows sin's grip to smithereens. By grace, we die with Jesus and wake up as a new person with an allergy to sin and an addiction to righteousness. Shocking, we know. That's why a person like this can handle total forgiveness, even of future sins. Why? Because they don't really *want* to sin anymore. That's key.

Remember, the Old Covenant was like a layaway plan for sin management—a never-ending cycle of IOUs to God, paid in livestock. Efficient? Not even close. Effective? Only in showing how desperately we needed a better deal. Enter Jesus, the show-stopping Lamb of God, whose solo performance on the cross closed the curtain on sin once and for all. No animal extras required. No sequel scheduled.

And yet, here we are, under the New Covenant, wringing our hands and wondering if Jesus's once-for-all forgiveness might be too good to be true. It's like we're waiting for Jesus to pop up like an arcade character and declare, "Surprise! Please request forgiveness for your most recent sin to continue playing the game."

Oh, and let's not forget the ultimate mic drop: Jesus didn't stick around for applause or encores. He sat down at the right hand of the Father, signaling the job was done and the victory won.

Despite this, the static of uncertainty still buzzes through our church speakers. It's like we've convinced ourselves that the cross was more of an opening act than the grand finale. This creates a culture of spiritual paranoia, where our status with God feels like a stock market crash waiting to happen, instead of the stone-solid guarantee it truly is.

So, to the pastors, teachers, and self-appointed gatekeepers of grace, we urge you: dust off those Bibles, dig through those concordances, and let's get back to the real deal. Preach the undiluted, scandalously generous grace of God—the kind that snaps chains, reshapes lives, and flings open prison doors.

To the guilt-ridden souls pacing our pews: take a deep breath, kick off those shoes of doubt, and collapse into the finished work of Christ. Your ticket's been punched, your debt's been paid, and your future's so bright, you'll need heavenly shades.

In a toast to the outrageous grace of our Lord,
Andronicus and Johannes, a couple of grace junkies spiking the communion juice

ONCE WAS ENOUGH!

To the Mosaic Magistrates of Modernity:

What a tangled web we weave when first we practice to . . . misunderstand grace. As self-appointed guardians of a grace that you fear will run amok, you've somehow managed to turn the liberating Gospel of Jesus Christ into a spiritual game of Simon Says, minus the fun.

Let's take a moment to step back into the bloody reality of the Old Testament—no PG rating here, folks. Hebrews 9 doesn't pull punches when reminding us that without a bloodbath, there's no mopping up of sins: "and without shedding of blood there is no forgiveness" (Hebrews 9:22b). But this wasn't some divine fascination with the macabre. It was a billboard-sized warning about the gravity of our rebellion and the staggering price tag for making things right.

Fast forward to the New Testament, and what do we have? The Ultimate Sacrifice. Jesus didn't whisper "It is finished" (John 19:30) like He was signing off after a boring shift at the office. No, this was the cosmic mic drop to end all cosmic mic drops. He wasn't just clocking out; He was shutting down the entire system of animal sacrifice, ushering in a new covenant of grace so profound, it's left us scratching our heads for millennia.

Now, here's where things get a bit sticky. Despite this game-changing event, our modern religious machinery seems determined to reboot the very cycle Christ obliterated. Both Team Catholic and Team Protestant, despite their rivalry in the theological Olympics, often fall into the same old trap: acting like Christ's one-time sacrifice was just the opening act for a never-ending spiritual circus of confession, penance, and begging for forgiveness. It's like we're trying to pay off grace on an installment plan, one Hail Mary or heartfelt "I'm sorry" at a time.

This relentless Do-It-Yourself forgiveness project not only misses the point but essentially tapes a "Kick Me" sign on the back of the gospel. Hebrews 10:14 couldn't be clearer: Jesus's one-time offering left us perfectly forgiven and perpetually cleansed, not stuck in some twisted game of Red Light, Green Light with our sins.

Yet, here we are, carting around our guilt like a badge of honor, as if every misstep requires a fresh dollop of forgiveness, personally FedExed by our groveling. This isn't humility; it's amnesia—forgetting that "It is finished" means exactly what it says. Our cleansing is a done deal, not a doorbuster sale where we camp out in front of the store hoping to grab a new slice of forgiveness every weekend.

Our stumbles should indeed grieve us—not because we fear we've knocked God's balance sheet off kilter, but because they remind us of the great love already poured out for us. And James 5:16's call to confess to one another isn't about unlocking forgiveness from God but about walking in honesty with others. It's not about a heavenly transaction but a relational benefit with trusted friends.

The idea that we're playing a game of forgiveness fetch—lobbing our sins up to God and hoping He throws back absolution—is a tragic misunderstanding. We're not forgiven because we're good at saying sorry; we're forgiven because He is extravagantly good. This isn't carte blanche to set world records for sin, but an invitation to live free, propelled by grace towards godliness. (Hint: When you know you're clean, you'll act clean.)

So, dear Church, let's wipe clear our theological glasses and take a long, hard look at the cross: the once-and-for-all bridge between our mess and His mercy. Our lives shouldn't reflect a frantic scramble for forgiveness but a joyful walk rooted in the rock-solid truth of our perpetual purity before God.

It really is finished,
Andronicus and Johannes

EPICENTERS OF DIVINE FORGETFULNESS

To the Architects of Tomorrow's Temples:

In a world teeming with transactional relationships and conditional love, the concept of "once and for all" forgiveness seems almost alien. Yet, herein lies the crux of our faith, the bedrock of belief, and the jailbreak of our souls.

It's not about the messes we've made since our last tearful confession or the sins we tally in moments of despair. No, it's about a grace so scandalous, so outrageous, that doubt is homeless, guilt is evicted, and the endless cycle of confess-cleanse-compromise gets a permanent shutdown.

Consider the sheer audacity of believing that our sins—past, present, and even the ones still incubating—are already accounted for, already forgiven, and utterly obliterated by the singular sacrifice of Calvary. This is not the stuff of legends or the whisperings of wishful thinkers. This is the bold declaration of Scripture, echoed in the halls of eternity and in the quiet of our hearts.

> "For Christ also died for sins *once for all*, the just for the unjust, so that He might bring us to God, having been put to death in the flesh, but made alive in the spirit." (1 Peter 3:18, emphasis added)

> "For by *one* offering He has perfected *for all time* those who are sanctified." (Hebrews 10:14, emphasis added)

Living in this shocking reality of forgiveness rebrands us from groveling sinners chasing absolution to saints anchored in Christ's unshakable righteousness. This is not a license for complacency but a call to live out our days in vibrant gratitude, propelled by the Spirit to embody the fruits of this profound truth. Imagine the freedom in knowing that our every misstep is not a bookkeeping entry requiring settlement but an opportunity to remember God's grace and align our thinking with His perspective.

Our failure to grip this truth fuels a vicious cycle of spiritual insecurity, where our standing with God feels as shaky as sandcastles at high tide. This outlook, often dramatized in the emotional crescendos of youth camp recommitments, distorts the beauty of God's grace into a Groundhog Day of seeking forgiveness. It turns our life in Christ into a task of perpetually pleading about sins already taken away forever.

Let this sink in: "As far as the east is from the west, so far has He removed our transgressions from us." (Psalm 103:12). Think about it—head east, and you'll keep going east forever; but go north, and soon enough, you're headed south. East and west never meet. That's how far gone your sins are—eternally out of reach, never circling back. That's not a polite gap—it's a cosmic chasm. We possess a freedom that invites us to live not as criminals on trial awaiting a verdict but as joyful heirs of an eternal kingdom.

With this in mind, our gatherings should explode as epicenters of grace, where the worn-out find rest, and the outcast and overlooked discover belonging. By embodying this grace, we counteract the world's narratives of conditional acceptance and performance-based worth. Let our churches be known not as courthouses of judgment but as banquet halls of mercy, where every heart is reminded of its value in the eyes of the One who calls us His own.

This brand of radical hospitality, rooted in our complete forgiveness, doesn't just transform communities—it gives them a sneak preview of Heaven.

Get this: Your sins aren't just forgiven—they're forgotten, washed away by the sea of God's unfathomable grace with no lifeline in sight. Our task now is not to rehash old failures or to live in a state of constant groveling but to embrace fully the freedom bought at such a high price.

Let's showcase the transformative power of a love so mind-bending, it transcends time, steamrolls sin, and dwarfs even our wildest dreams.

In His boundless love,
Andronicus and Johannes

CONFESSION OBSESSION

To the Gold-Plated Pharisees of Our Time and the Tearful Travelers on Their Turnpike:

In an age where Scripture is brandished with the fervor of a sword fight at dawn, it's tragicomically ironic how its core messages get twisted into pretzels of theological contortion. The doctrine of total forgiveness—simple in its profundity, profound in its simplicity—has been given the Cinderella treatment, scrubbing the floors while its stepsisters, Self-Effort and Guilt, hog the spotlight.

Let's slice through the theological jungle with a machete of context and clarity, shall we? The foot-washing fiesta in John 13, often hijacked to promote a doctrine of partial cleansing before God, instead showcases Jesus's masterclass in humility. "If I then, the Lord and the Teacher, washed your feet, you also ought to wash one another's feet" (John 13:14). This isn't about scrubbing our spiritual toenails ad infinitum—it's about stepping into Jesus's shoes of servant leadership.

Now, cue the dramatic music for the entrance of 1 John 1:9—the verse always charting as the number one hit from the ever-popular band, Twisted Scripture.

> If we confess our sins, He is faithful and righteous to forgive us our sins and to cleanse us from all unrighteousness. (1 John 1:9)

Context clues reveal this verse as John's rant against Gnosticism's sin-denial, not some revolving door of forgiveness for the already redeemed. John's not prescribing a daily cleanup on aisle 4 but affirming the one-and-done cleansing power of Jesus's sacrifice.

And let's not forget to tip our hats to the Gnostics, those pioneers of "alternative facts," whose sin-denial required a direct reality check from our guy, John:

- "If we say that we have no sin, we are deceiving ourselves and the truth is not in us." (1:8)
- "If we say that we have not sinned, we make Him a liar and His word is not in us." (1:10)

It's crystal clear from the surrounding verses that John wasn't setting up a spiritual hamster wheel for Christians to confess endlessly. Instead, he was flinging open the door to total forgiveness for Gnostic sin-deniers lurking outside. If they'll just get on the same page with God about their sinfulness (instead of pulling a full-on denial), they'll get the full pardon—wiped clean of *all* unrighteousness. Don't sleep on that little word "all" in 1 John 1:9—it's the linchpin of the whole deal. Total forgiveness of all sins is John's headline offer here—a guilt-erasing forgiveness package, the same one we believers already snagged in Christ.

Now, about that famous "confession tango"—that misinterpreted two-step suggesting we need to boogie down the confession line to keep the forgiveness flowing. But the New Testament plays a different tune: our sins—past, present, and future—wiped away are part of the all-inclusive package deal known as The Finished Work.

But the "Progressive Forgiveness Theory" suggests we're in a perpetual state of spiritual layaway, chipping away at our sin debt one confession at a time. But this theory flops harder than a box office bomb, ignoring the Scripture marquee of Hebrews 10:14, Ephesians 1:7, and Colossians 1:14, which flash our all-expenses-paid forgiveness in neon lights.

If we've been led to believe our spiritual journey resembles an endless game of "Sin and Tell," we're not playing by the Gospel's rules but by those of a game rigged against us. The truth? Our forgiveness isn't dangling from the fragile thread of our memory-and-confession acrobatics. No, it's not about our legal pad and our many words; it's about His cross and His blood.

Understanding this shifts our confession from a desperate plea for more forgiveness to a heartfelt "thank you" for the complete forgiveness we've already received. It turns our spiritual walk from a guilt-laden slog to a gratitude-fueled strut.

Let's not be like theological hoarders clinging to dusty doctrines that dim the brilliant light of the Gospel. Instead, may our churches become lighthouses of hope, grace, and unconditional love, guiding the weary and the lost to the safe harbor of Christ's cross. In a spirit of joyous rebellion against the chains of incomplete forgiveness, let's embark on this journey of rediscovery together.

May you bask in an abundance of grace and find yourself lounging in a lavish lack of legalism,
Andronicus and Johannes

GOD FORGIVES NICE PEOPLE?

To the Custodians of the Cross Confusing Converts Caught in the Crossfire:

Greetings from the fringes of your meticulously manicured spiritual lawns! In your valiant quest to polish the exterior of the cup and plate, you've somehow neglected the feast of grace laid out before you. Instead, you serve up the same old dish: conditional forgiveness, drizzled with a bitter glaze of legalistic rituals that Jesus Himself would find hard to stomach. So, let's cut into the meat of the matter, slicing through the gristle of confusion with the razor-sharp knife of Scripture.

First on the chopping block is that thorny chunk nestled in the Lord's Prayer (Matthew 6:14–15): "For if you forgive others for their transgressions, your heavenly Father will also forgive you. But if you do not forgive others, then your Father will not forgive your transgressions." This little gem is usually the ammunition of choice for guilt-ridden sermons designed to keep the flock on a short leash of moral reciprocity. But has it crossed your mind that Jesus wasn't laying down some divine "you scratch My back, I'll scratch yours" policy under the new covenant?

Let's sprinkle a bit of context seasoning here, shall we? Jesus, talking to an Old Covenant crowd, was essentially holding up a mirror to reveal the impossibility of earning forgiveness through human effort. The Sermon on the Mount, from which the Lord's Prayer sprouts, is a masterclass in setting the bar so astronomically high that even the most athletic Pharisee couldn't pole vault over it. His words on forgiveness? Not a decree, but a diagnosis—a divine X-ray exposing humanity's spiritual bankruptcy.

Now, fast forward to the New Covenant, delivered through the blood of Christ, where forgiveness isn't a commodity to be bartered with but a gift to be received. Under the new, Ephesians 4:32 and Colossians 3:13 flip the script. They don't dangle our forgiveness on the hook of "forgive first, then get forgiven"—quite the opposite!

> Be kind to one another, tender-hearted, forgiving each other, just as God in Christ also has forgiven you. (Ephesians 4:32)

> bearing with one another, and forgiving each other, whoever has a complaint against anyone; just as the Lord forgave you, so also should you. (Colossians 3:13)

These verses invite us to forgive, not to earn God's forgiveness, but as an overflow of the forgiveness we've *already* been given by Him. It's a heart so full it spills over. It's not a spiritual *quid pro quo.*

So, let's take a scalpel to the Lord's Prayer, shall we? Jesus, in His pre-cross days, was talking to a crowd tangled in the Old Covenant's catch-22 of conditional blessings and curses. His prayer wasn't a carrot-and-stick routine for us New Covenant folks; it was a teaching tool, pointing straight to the failure of self-righteousness and the desperate need for a Savior. In other words, "Imagine only being forgiven to the degree you've forgiven others. Newsflash: You'd be toast!"

Pivoting to unconditional forgiveness in the New Covenant? It's like trading a tricycle for a jet plane. Why wobble through life on the shaky wheels of self-effort when you've got the Spirit's wings to lift you into the heights of grace? Hebrews 10:14 and other towering Scriptures guide us away from the rocky shores of "forgiveness if you're nice first" to the calm waters of "forgiveness finished once and for all."

Let's not beat around the bush: the recipe for spiritual life needs the right ingredients. In Christ, our forgiveness is not a daily bread we must bake with the yeast of our many confessions. No, it's a full banquet, already laid out. All that's left for us to do is sit back, feast, and revel in the Chef's generosity.

Bon appétit! And remember—your tab's already covered. Let's not insult the Chef by trying to scrub the dishes afterward.

Your fellow banqueters,
Andronicus and Johannes

IN-N-OUT THEOLOGY

To the Front Pew Dwellers and the Heavy-Hearted Haulers of Holiness:

A crucial truth has been buried in translation: the breathtaking reality of our unbreakable fellowship with God through Jesus Christ. So, let's put our current state under the microscope.

First up, the much-debated topic of repentance—a term that, for all its airtime, might as well be a Shakespearean sonnet recited backward for how badly it's misunderstood. Some voices act like any mention of sin struggle is practically high treason against Christ's sacrifice. Let's clear the fog: recognizing and turning from sin doesn't undermine Calvary—it magnifies it!

But repentance isn't about punching a timecard to keep the heavenly forgiveness meter ticking. It's a mental U-turn, sparked by a glimpse of our righteousness and God's overwhelming goodness. It's not a denial of the "once for all" efficacy of Jesus's work (Hebrews 10:10–14), but a heartfelt response to it. We confess, not to activate forgiveness, but out of the overflow of a new heart: a pristine heart that detests evil and is grateful for the forgiveness we already possess.

And then there's godly sorrow (2 Corinthians 7:10), which has been miscast as badly as a villain in a soap opera. It's not about throwing ourselves into a pit of despair but realizing our actions grieve the Spirit who's already embraced us tighter than ever. Our sorrow isn't the currency we trade for forgiveness; it's the natural response of new-hearted children who love their Father and regret the pain they may have caused others. Let's make it plain: There are truckloads of reasons to turn from sin, but squeezing out more forgiveness from God isn't one of them!

Now for the controversy over fellowship with God—a concept as twisted as a tabloid headline: Hebrews 10:14 makes it crystal that our fellowship with God isn't a yo-yo on the string of our moral performance. It is a secure connection established by Christ's definitive work on the cross. If sin could really sever our fellowship with God, then the cross is nothing more than a cosmic Band-Aid, and Christ's triumphant "It is finished" (John 19:30) is nothing but wishful thinking.

The tale some spin that we fall in and out of fellowship with God isn't just unbiblical—it's heresy wrapped in a religious disguise. Romans 8:38–39 doesn't come with a footnote excluding sin from the list of things unable to separate us from God's love. Our standing before God isn't based on our spiritual acrobatics but on Christ's irrefutable performance.

Why do we turn from sin? Not out of a trembling fear of losing God's favor (a favor never predicated on our purity to begin with), but from a place of profound gratitude and love for the One who called us His own. And how would we ever turn from sin anyway if we were "out of fellowship" with God? We'd have no power to do so! But thank God we're permanently glued to Christ. We're dead to sin, and at our core, we loathe it. We're above sin, too good for it. Sin is beneath us—where it belongs. Don't let anyone tell you differently.

Let's jettison the tired tropes of conditional forgiveness and falling in-and-out of fellowship. Instead, let's grab hold of the wild, liberating truth of the Gospel: in Christ, we're forgiven—completely and forever. Our fellowship with God is not a prize to be won or lost but a gift to be enjoyed. We are swimming in a river of God's goodness, not trembling on a tightrope. So ditch the spiritual high wire act, and let's cannonball into the deep end of grace!

May our lives, then, be a joyful ode to the freedom we have in Christ as we dance in the delight of our Father's unchanging love.

In unbreakable fellowship with God,
Andronicus and Johannes, boycotting the in-n-out burger

TWO GROUPS, ONE JUDGMENT

To the Librarians of the Law and the Tired Travelers Awaiting Their Trial:

Judgment Day shouldn't have us quaking in our boots. We ought to be standing tall, buzzing with excitement, in the love of Christ that kicks fear to the curb. It's not about acing some divine report card; it's about kicking back in the perfect work of Jesus on the cross. Yes, we can be oozing confidence on that day:

> . . . we may have confidence in the day of judgment; because as He is, so also are we in this world. There is no fear in love; but perfect love casts out fear, because fear involves punishment, and the one who fears is not perfected in love. (1 John 4:17b–18)

If we're freaking out over the final judgment, it's because we've been duped into expecting punishment. But there's no punishment left for us, period (John 3:18; Romans 8:1). The wages of sin is death. Jesus died. Do the math and celebrate.

Now, the judgment seat of Christ (see 2 Corinthians 5:10) is often billed as some celestial talent show where believers get trophies or a slap on the wrist for their life's performance. But this misses the entire rhythm of God's kingdom. This judgment is more like a grand reveal, a final spotlight showing lives either in sync with the Gospel or hopelessly out of tune. It's not a separate encore for believers but the same main event where everyone—believers and unbelievers—takes the stage. This is precisely why it says we must *all* appear at the judgment seat of Christ. "All" means all humans, not just believers:

> For we must all appear before the judgment seat of Christ, so that each one may be recompensed for his deeds in the body, according to what he has done, whether good or bad. (2 Corinthians 5:10)

Believers get rewarded simply for being in Christ (and even if they've only handed out a cup of water in His name!), while unbelievers? Well, they're left to face the music for every single deed. This passage has to be about all humans. Why? Because only believers have good deeds done in the body, and only unbelievers have bad deeds they'll be recompensed (paid back) for.

Similarly, the sheep and goats parable (see Matthew 25) isn't some side act—it's part of the same story, separating those who groove to the melody of grace from those playing their own offbeat tune.

There is much confusion suggesting that believers and unbelievers will attend separate judgments, yet the Scriptures reveal a single, majestic event. The passages in Matthew 25, Revelation 20–21, and

2 Corinthians 5:10, when conducted together, unveil the Great White Throne, the *bema* (which coincidentally, is great and white), as the singular platform for judgment and reward.

You won't be answering for your sins, because Jesus already did. Paid. In. Full. Game over. It is finished. This grand finale drowns the fear of judgment in a raucous chorus of celebration, locking in the all-encompassing victory that Jesus pulled off on the cross.

As for this idea that believers will collect different rewards based on how well they performed on Earth? The parable of the vineyard workers (Matthew 20:1–16) blows that myth to pieces, showcasing God's grace as the ultimate equalizer. Some clocked in at sunrise, others with only an hour to spare, and guess what? Everyone got the same paycheck. Our reward, dear friends, is not a collection of heavenly trophies but Christ Himself—our priceless treasure. Philippians 3:8 echoes this, reminding us that everything else is dung (here, we're keeping it clean) compared to knowing Christ.

Some folks like to picture this world as a stage where God's constantly dishing out judgments left and right. But even our present sufferings and global tumults are not acts of divine retribution but the birth pains of a creation yearning for redemption. So let's stop living like actors on some audition stage, and start living like beloved children who know the Conductor has already given us a standing ovation.

May our lives reflect not a fearful anticipation of judgment but a joyful expectation of the day when every tear will be wiped away, and we will dwell in perfect harmony with our Maker forever.

In a peculiar confidence some misinterpret as arrogance,
Andronicus and Johannes, co-judges with you of the world and the
angels (1 Corinthians 6:2–3)

INHERITANCES AREN'T EARNED

To the Tradition-Trapped Taskmasters and Their Troupe:

It seems a clarification is direly needed to cut through the fog of your reward-based theology.

The bustling marketplace of spiritual merit badges you've set up suggests a heavenly ledger where deeds are currency and salvation's just another stock in your portfolio. But this celestial Wall Street crashes hard against the Gospel's core—grace, not spiritual sweat equity.

Let's sift through the New Testament, where—surprise!—it speaks not of a buffet of rewards but one colossal prize. In Philippians 3:8, Paul shouts, "I count all things to be loss in view of the surpassing value of knowing Christ Jesus my Lord, for whom I have suffered the loss of all things, and count them but rubbish so that I may gain Christ." The apostle calls everything else garbage compared to the gem of knowing Christ. So, if you're banking on stacking up spiritual trophies, you're dealing in the wrong currency.

And remember what we already highlighted in our previous letter: Jesus's parable in Matthew 20:1–16 doesn't leave much room for ambiguity. The vineyard workers all punched out with the same paycheck, no matter how many hours they clocked. This isn't a tale of economic injustice. It's a divine comedy about grace, poking fun at our obsession with fairness. If Heaven doesn't operate on a punch clock, why are we checking in and out, expecting overtime pay?

And next, we must tackle 1 Corinthians 3, a favorite haunt for those eager to tally celestial rewards. Paul's metaphor of building on the foundation of Christ isn't an invitation to a reward banquet but a stern warning about the importance of wielding an accurate gospel:

- "I planted, Apollos watered" (3:6)
- "For we are God's fellow workers" (3:9)
- "I laid a foundation" (3:10a)
- "and another is building on it" (3:10b)
- "each man must be careful how he builds on it" (3:10c)
- "each man's work will become evident" (3:13a)
- "fire itself will test the quality of each man's work" (3:13b)
- "if any man's work . . . remains, he will receive a reward" (3:14)
- "If any man's work is burned up, he will suffer loss" (3:15)

Picture this: the pyrotechnics of God's judgment torch the false teachings of deceivers, leaving only what's genuinely built on Christ. This isn't a celestial bonfire of lost rewards for believers but a cleansing blaze that incinerates the works of false teachers. Here, God is simply upholding the purity of His truth. It's about God's disdain for deception, not a stingy handout of heavenly prizes.

Plus, Colossians 3:23–24 introduces a real twist: "the reward of the inheritance." Um, hello? An inheritance isn't earned; someone dies and leaves it to you. So, it's not about climbing the spiritual corporate ladder but about what Christ has already accomplished through His death. This inheritance isn't a collection of certificates redeemable in Heaven's gift shop—it's an unspoiled reward waiting for *every* believer. Yes, all, because Jesus died and gave it to us as an inheritance. In fact, we are *co-heirs* with Christ (Romans 8:17)!

Now, about those crowns—the Scriptures do mention shiny headpieces, but to imagine them as tangible rewards we collect is to miss the point. These aren't victory laps for our achievements; they're symbols of what we already have in Christ: life, glory, and righteousness. He is our ultimate crown. (Note: That's why the twenty-four elders in Revelation toss their crowns like frisbees at the feet of Jesus.)

Consider the vine-branches dynamic in John 15—it's the final nail in the coffin for the level-up theology of bigger mansions and bling. If our spiritual fruitfulness stems from Christ within us (and apart from Him, we've got *zilch*), then the idea of earning an assortment of rewards based on our actions starts to look rather silly, don't you think? Our deeds are the byproduct of His work in us, not a spiritual résumé to be graded.

It's time to ditch this fantasy faith where God's a cosmic vending machine and embrace the reality: Christ is the treasure. Our inheritance isn't a piecemeal collection of celestial knick-knacks but a shared destiny with Christ, secured by grace.

We can shed the spiritual capitalism that has entangled our understanding of reward. We're called to take hold of the liberating truth: the treasure isn't scattered across Heaven waiting to be unearthed based on our spiritual performance. It's Christ Himself, our source of eternal joy. After all, to live is Christ, and to die is gain (Philippians 1:21). So, let's stop scavenging for spiritual trinkets and start reveling in the true treasure—Christ Himself, our ultimate inheritance.

May this truth inspire us to serve not for the sake of heavenly loot but out of love for our Savior.

With a glance toward the true treasure,
Andronicus and Johannes

EXAMINATION INFESTATION

To the Sacramental Supervisors and the Sighing Standers-By:

It's time to tackle an issue that's been gnawing at the soul of our collective gatherings—the observance of the Lord's Supper. Imagine this: a celebration gone sour, a feast hijacked by funeral vibes, where joy is eclipsed by a fog of guilt and self-reproach. Have we not veered from the feast Jesus envisioned?

Let's talk about Paul and those rowdy Corinthians, shall we? When Paul urged them to "examine themselves" before diving into the bread and wine (1 Corinthians 11:28), it seems the memo got lost in translation. Paul wasn't running a sin-audit seminar. He was tackling a more pressing banquet-specific disaster: the spectacle of people getting plastered and hoarding all the bread, leaving nothing for the poor or the fashionably late. It's like showing up to a potluck armed with just a fork, contributing nothing, and then devouring the entire casserole, solo. Paul's call for self-examination was a plea for some basic table manners, not a spiritual scorecard. It was about making sure the table remained a place of unity, not division—or drunken debauchery.

The irony of today's pre-communion navel-gazing is too rich to ignore. We're busy scrutinizing every flaw, jumping through self-imposed hoops, to qualify for a feast that's practically screaming, "He qualified you!" The Lord's Supper is the ultimate banquet of grace, but here we are, twisting ourselves in knots, questioning our worthiness to partake in a feast that is meant to celebrate our place at the table. It's like being the guest of honor but hesitating at the door, worried your shoes aren't fancy enough to get in.

And then we've got the ritual—a pre-communion guilt-a-thon, justified by one misinterpreted "examination" sentence from Paul (1 Corinthians 11:28). What's really happening in that passage? Even a quick glance reveals there are "divisions" and "factions" among them, because some are selfishly eating and drinking everything up before others show up. As a result, they need to examine their selfish practices and "wait for one another":

- "divisions exist among you" (11:18)
- "factions among you" (11:19)
- "one takes his own supper first" (11:21)
- "one is hungry and another is drunk" (11:21)
- "shame those who have nothing" (11:22)
- "whoever eats the bread or drinks the cup of the Lord in an unworthy manner" (11:27)
- "But a man must examine himself . . ." (11:28)
- "when you come together to eat, wait for one another" (11:33)

What's the "unworthy manner"? Stuffing your face and not waiting for everyone else! Looks like we've mistaken a community feast for a personal pity party. Paul was dealing with community conduct, not handing out tickets for a guilt trip. This was never about dimming the lights, cueing the sad music, and inspecting your latest sins like a bad highlight reel. The real irony? This introspection misses the entire point of the celebration: Christ's sacrifice, not our sin inventory. So, why are we trying to qualify for a feast that's literally designed to celebrate the fact that He already qualified us?

Of course, some folks trot out Matthew 5:24 like it's the golden ticket for their pre-communion clean-up routine:

> leave your offering there before the altar and go; first be reconciled to your brother, and then come and present your offering. (Matthew 5:24)

But, my friends, this is apples to oranges. Jesus was talking to the proud Jews of His day, calling out their hypocrisy—offering animal sacrifices while nursing grudges—not giving instructions for the communion table. And let's not forget that, at the Lord's Supper, you don't offer anything; you celebrate the sacrifice Christ offered!

The Lord's Supper isn't a time for a self-pity spiral but a moment to bask in the blazing light of grace, celebrating not our introspective moral gymnastics but Christ's all-encompassing victory. This is not about us trying to be worthy but about Christ having made us worthy. We're not solitary sin managers but a family, united under the banner of grace, called to live this out in love and forgiveness.

So, let's finally ditch this "get right in three minutes or less before the Welch's and the Wonder Bread arrive at your row." Instead, let's see communion as the appetizer for the grand banquet in the Kingdom. That's how we reclaim the Lord's Supper for what it really is—a celebration of grace and a sneak peek of the glory to come. Let's gather not as mourners clutching tissues, but as celebrants raising glasses, united in grace and grinning at the feast ahead.

Picture us clinking our glasses with yours,
Andronicus and Johannes

CATACLYSMS AND CATECHISMS

To the Peddlers of Piety and the Wounded Walkers in the Wilderness:

Disasters flood our feeds every day, from bone-chilling terror to earth-shaking calamities. Some among us have donned a prophet's mantle, declaring these events as the Almighty's thunderous rebuke of humanity's blunders. This stance, though wrapped in a veneer of holy insight, sadly paints our God as a tyrant eager to smite and slow to soothe.

Did we lose the memo on God's character somewhere along the way? Scripture sketches a radically different picture of our Father. Far from being the cosmic disciplinarian, our God is a paragon of patience and a champion of second chances.

Hurricanes. Terror attacks. Global pandemics. The skewed notion that each disaster is some kind of divine spanking for our naughtiness has wormed its way into our belief system. Not only does this clash with everything Jesus stands for, but it also mangles His very essence. Scripture couldn't be clearer: God is not on a destruction spree—He's more like a Father standing at the door, heart in hand, waiting for us to knock (2 Peter 3:9; 1 Timothy 2:3–4).

Enter Jesus, the flesh-and-blood mirror of God's heart. He didn't hand out judgments like candy—He handed out healing, forgiveness, and life. His days on Earth were proof of a God who weeps with us in our sorrow and seeks to mend, not maim.

Don't be fooled: the catastrophes and sicknesses that plague our world aren't heavenly missiles; they're fallout from a world knocked off its axis. Even Jesus made it clear—trouble is the hallmark of this planet, but He offers peace in the storm (John 16:33).

Wielding Old Testament verses like 2 Chronicles 7:14 as a one-size-fits-all lens for today's disasters? That's like using a Chinese compass from 200 BC to navigate a Tesla. But, for the enthusiasts, here's the verse for your viewing pleasure:

> "and My people who are called by My name humble themselves and pray and seek My face and turn from their wicked ways, then I will hear from heaven, will forgive their sin and will heal their land."

It's our go-to verse for every disaster, like a magic spell we think will fix everything. "Maybe if our leaders would just hit the floor and repent, God would put a stop to this crisis." Newsflash: God didn't bring it upon us, and He never promised we'd be free from it—at least, not before we hit Heaven's gate.

All this presumption disregards the new covenant Jesus brought in, making God look like He's itching to hit the smite button. Jesus Himself said, "for I did not come to judge the world, but to save the world." (John 12:47). So, what's changed? Yes, judgment day is coming—but guess what? It's not today!

Thinking disasters are God's way of slapping our wrists? That's not just a misfire on God's character—it cheapens the whole Gospel. We're not living in a time of wrath; we're living in an era of salvation. The door's wide open to grace (2 Corinthians 6:2). Our story is one of hope, not doom and gloom.

Yes, a final reckoning is on the docket—it's in the Book. But right now, our present call is to live in the light of God's grace, extending that same grace-filled invite through faith in Jesus. This shift in thinking pushes us to drop the finger-wagging and embrace the world with wide-open arms of love and compassion.

Our mission, should we choose to accept it, is to smash the myths about God that breed fear. Let's rewrite the narrative—one of a Father yearning for everyone to taste the freedom found in His truth.

Celebrating the healthy view of our God,
Andronicus and Johannes

HINDERING GOD

To the Legionnaires of the Letter and their Fragile Followers Fumbling for Freedom:

Let's cut to the chase and dive into the much-misunderstood dynamics of our relationship with the Holy Spirit. First up: "Do not quench the Spirit" (1 Thessalonians 5:19a).

Imagine, if you will, the Holy Spirit as a roaring flame within you—lighting your way, energizing your soul. Quenching this flame doesn't bring God's wrath but thwarts the very expression of our new nature. It's like wearing winter clothes on a sunny beach; it clashes with who you really are now. You were designed to bask in the Spirit's warmth, to sync up with His rhythm, not to smother His effect under the soggy blanket of your old ways.

Then there's the tender twist: "Do not grieve the Holy Spirit of God" (Ephesians 4:30). But grieving here doesn't mean stirring up God's anger. Nope, the cross has extinguished that firestorm for good. Instead, it's more like the heartache of a parent watching their kid stumble. It's a love story, not a guilt trip—proof of God's intimate involvement in your life, His burning desire for you to live in the full joy and freedom He signed in blood at Calvary. Grieving the Spirit is less about incurring God's displeasure and more about going against your very nature—like a fish deciding to take up mountain climbing. You were built to glide in grace, not slog in sin.

And then there's that old sowing and reaping business in Galatians 6. Well, it's not a threat but a loving reminder of your profound transformation. You're dead to sin and magnificently alive to God—allergic to sin and hopelessly addicted to Jesus. Sowing to the flesh? About as satisfying as chewing on cardboard for lunch—utterly lacking in flavor and nourishment. Your new heart craves the rich expressions of the Spirit, for in displaying them, you're being the most authentic version of you.

When you sow to the Spirit, you're not striving for approval or laboring under the weight of obligation. Rather, you're dancing in rhythm with your truest identity, relishing in the deeds and desires that resonate with your "new self." It's about fulfillment, not obligation; identity, not duty. The harvest you reap from walking by the Spirit—life, peace, and joy—is not just your reward; it's the natural expression of your new spiritual DNA.

So, quenching and grieving the Spirit? It's not about invoking God's wrath—it's about the jarring dissonance you experience when you stray from what you actually love. It's God's kindness leading you back to reality—a divine nudge reminding you of who you are—but it's also your own self craving to return to what makes you happy.

Your missteps don't trigger God's fury; they trigger a Father's longing for you to thrive in the life He's given you. Every moment, you're invited to live out this Spirit-filled adventure, to echo Heaven's heartbeat here on Earth.

May our lives be a festival of freedom, celebrating Him in us and us in Him.

Walking by the Spirit,
Andronicus and Johannes

THE UNFORGIVABLE MYTH

To the Scribes of Scorn and the Bruised Believers on the Bench:

Welcome to the rollercoaster of theological acrobatics, where the truth often gets tangled in a web of well-intentioned but wildly misguided interpretations. Let's dive straight into the deep end, shall we? We're tackling the misunderstood blockbuster of the theological world: the so-called "unforgivable sin." Grab your popcorn.

Jesus dropped a bombshell when He spoke about blasphemy against the Holy Spirit:

> "Therefore I say to you, any sin and blasphemy shall be forgiven people, but blasphemy against the Spirit shall not be forgiven." (Matthew 12:31)

Now, this isn't your garden-variety slip-up. It's not about cussing God out or pulling a reckless stunt like suicide and waiting for divine thunderbolts. No, blasphemy against the Holy Spirit is the endgame of rejection—the full-throttle decision to turn your back on the offer of salvation, Jesus Himself. It's the hardcore denial of the person and work of Jesus, earning exclusive membership to the "I Reject the Truth" club.

Now, let's get real about suicide, often miscast as the unforgivable sin *du jour*. Plain and simple: Scripture doesn't back this up. John's letter simply points out the difference between rejecting Christ (big no-no) and every other mistake under the sun: a "sin leading to death" versus "a sin not leading to death" (1 John 5:16).

Equating suicide with the ultimate unforgivable sin isn't just sloppy theology; it's spiritual malpractice. Are we seriously suggesting that God abandons depressed Christians at their lowest? Please. It's the opposite: He *grieves* with those who grieve (see Romans 12:15).

So, let's quit the bad PR campaign. Stop treating God's grace like a fragile Fabergé egg, shattering at the slightest touch. The idea that a fleeting moment of despair could cut someone off from His eternal mercy? That's a gross misreading of the Gospel's heartbeat. Our God isn't waiting at the pearly gates with a checklist, ready to turn away the brokenhearted. He's the Shepherd leaving the ninety-nine to search for the one.

The real deal-breaker? Unbelief. That's the sin with the real sting, the flat-out refusal to grab the lifeline that's right in front of you. That's the cliff edge where eternal separation starts, not in the million and one ways we find to screw up.

It's time to ditch the doom and gloom narrative and get back to the liberating truth of God's goodness. We're not in the condemnation business—we're here to broadcast hope from the rooftops. The Gospel is about love, not loopholes, and there's always a way back from the brink.

Let's be clear: our standing with God isn't about stamina; it's about the gift we've already received through faith in Christ. "For by one offering He has perfected forever those who are sanctified" (Hebrews 10:14). (Fun fact: There's no fine print.)

So, why peddle fear when we're meant to mirror Jesus, arms wide open to those teetering on the edge of despair? Remember: It's all about God's grace—no asterisks needed.

In Christ's Unstoppable Love,
Andronicus and Johannes

Let's be [illegible] about standing with God [illegible] about grammar [illegible] the gift we've already received through faith in Christ. "For by one offering He has perfected forever those who are sanctified" (Hebrews 10:14 [illegible]). That's good news, man.

So why peddle [illegible] a counterfeit gospel? [illegible] wide open [illegible] on the edge of despair [illegible] about God's grace—in a [illegible].

In Christ's Unstoppable Love,
[illegible]

PART 4

DIVINE ENTWINE

TAKING THE PLUNGE

To the Drenched Devotees of Doctrine, the Soggy Saints, and their Sprinkled Siblings:

Let's cannonball off the high dive right into the splash zone of baptism. Now, don't kid yourself: this isn't just another item on the agenda. It's the heavyweight champion of church debates, where opinions are as plentiful (and flavored) as the coffee in the foyer.

Brace yourselves for a shocking revelation: salvation isn't a membership card you earn by taking a dip in the holy jacuzzi. Astonishing, we know. The idea that one must perform the aquatic ballet to secure a spot in eternity is as bewildering as it is biblically baseless.

Are we really to believe that the Almighty's master plan hinges on whether you've had your underwater moment? That Heaven's gates are propped open by a few gallons of water? Perish the thought, and let's not slip into the idolatry of worshiping the created (water) over the Creator (God).

Let's wade a little deeper, shall we? Water baptism is a stunning Instagram snapshot of what's already gone down in your human spirit: a symbolic selfie of your death, burial, and resurrection with Christ. But make no mistake—it's the Spirit's work inside you, not the water outside, that saves.

The Scriptures are crystal on this one. Remember the thief on the cross? No baptismal certificate, yet Jesus personally reserved his spot in Paradise (Luke 23:39–43). And those Spirit-filled Gentiles in Acts 10? They broke protocol, getting the Spirit *before* taking the plunge: "Surely no one can refuse the water for these to be baptized who have received the Holy Spirit just as we did, can he?" (verse 47). Then there's Paul, the jet-setting apostle, who didn't treat baptism like the golden ticket: "For Christ did not send me to baptize, but to preach the gospel" (1 Corinthians 1:17a). Paul was all about the message of Jesus crucified and raised—not *The Gospel According to Aquaman*.

Elevating ritual over relationship? That's like putting ketchup on filet mignon—it's just wrong. To insist water baptism is a must for salvation is to imply Christ's death and resurrection were just appetizers, and now we need to order the main course. Let's not confuse the dip for the divine DNA swap.

For those clinging to baptism like it's a spiritual life jacket, remember: we're saved by submitting to the grace of Christ, not by performing rituals. Baptism isn't being benched on the sidelines—it's just not the game-winning play. It's the victory lap, not the race itself.

In the grand tapestry of faith, let's not get tangled in the threads of legalism. Water baptism is the public shout-out, not your secret access code to Heaven. Born of water (pro tip: think childbirth) and the Spirit (spiritual rebirth)—salvation is about what's happened inside, not the splash on the outside (John 3:5–6).

So, let's not mistake the shadow for the substance. Our salvation isn't sealed by a baptismal dunk but by being plunged into the Spirit through faith in Jesus. It's time to celebrate our true immersion in Christ's love, not merely our dip in the pool.

Have you overplayed the ritual and downplayed your new spiritual location? Baptism's a beautiful symbol, but it's not the substance of your salvation. Rejoice in your union with Christ, secured by faith and stamped by the Holy Spirit. Celebrate water baptism as a testimony, not a ticket.

And please, share this with those still wet behind the ears.

Andronicus and Johannes, damp disciples of the Divine

LIVING PROOF

To the Shadows Shivering at the Sermons:

Eternal life—it's not a fast-pass to the great beyond nor a distant dream to cling to. It's not your old life with a heavenly facelift. It's not your former life with an extended warranty. Nope, it's the pulsating new life of Christ within us, right here, right now.

"Because I live, you will live also," Jesus quipped (John 14:19). Eternal life isn't about punching the clock for eternity; it's about the up-close, personal presence of Jesus—our walking, talking salvation. If you've got Him, you've got eternal life:

- "He who has the Son has the life." (1 John 5:12)
- "We shall be saved by His life." (Romans 5:10)

Now, here's a myth more stubborn than leftover holiday weight—the idea that you can own salvation but only rent the Holy Spirit on a trial basis. Scripture laughs in the face of such folly, insisting that snagging Christ means also snagging His Spirit in full—no assembly required: "But if anyone does not have the Spirit of Christ, he does not belong to Him" (Romans 8:9b). You're complete in Him, already equipped for every spiritual escapade:

- "in Him you have been made complete" (Colossians 2:10)
- "His divine power has granted to us everything pertaining to life and godliness" (2 Peter 1:3)
- Christ "has blessed us with every spiritual blessing" (Ephesians 1:3)

So, where is our true calling found? Not in spiritual calisthenics but in the effortless dance of faith, intertwined with Christ. Married to Him, we don't tick religious boxes—we bear fruit (see Romans 7:4). Trying to crank out fruit without Him? It's as futile as trying to tan in a thunderstorm. This is about basking in His presence, not hustling for His approval.

Now, for a classic trap: the endless chase for spiritual upgrades, like the Gospel's some smartphone needing constant downloads. This mentality belittles the grandeur of what we've already inherited in Christ—a reality where we lack nothing. We're called not to collect new spiritual toys but to dive into the vast riches we already have.

The heartbeat of our faith isn't a perk for the spiritually elite but a gift for everyone—the indwelling Christ, our hope and glory (Colossians 1:27). So, why sweat under the crushing weight of spiritual performance when we can rest in the sufficiency of His grace, letting the natural overflow of union with Him produce fruit?

We're branches grafted into the Vine, not solo performers on a spiritual stage. Our lives reflect His love, not our efforts. It's not about spiritual heroics; it's the effortless flow of His life through us:

> "I am the vine, you are the branches; he who abides in Me and I in him, he bears much fruit, for apart from Me you can do nothing." (John 15:5)

> "Come to Me, all who are weary and heavy-laden, and I will give you rest. Take My yoke upon you and learn from Me, for I am gentle and humble in heart, and you will find rest for your souls. For My yoke is easy and My burden is light." (Matthew 11:28–30)

Think of it as spiritual osmosis—no striving, just absorption. So, why settle for commemorating Easter once a year when you can live the resurrection daily, embracing the electric vitality of Christ's life within you? The cross wasn't the finish line—it was just the starting gun. Your salvation is as enduring as the resurrection life of Jesus (Hebrews 7:25), and that truth should energize you more than a triple shot of espresso.

Always remember: You're not just forgiven; you're fundamentally transformed. You're not just twiddling your thumbs, waiting for eternal life— you're living it, in Christ, right now. Let this profound reality ignite your understanding, emboldening you to showcase the resurrection life of Jesus every single day.

Spreading the scandal of grace,
Andronicus and Johannes

FREE JESUS

To the Pulpit Protectors and Their Chapel Champions:

We dispatch this message to address one of the most ironic errors plaguing believers today: the never-ending quest to "get closer" to God. It appears many of us have been led astray by the distressing belief that our spiritual proximity to the Almighty waxes and wanes like the moon, contingent upon our religious labor.

Let's be abundantly clear: In Christ, you're already as snug with God as you're ever going to be. This isn't the fruit of your spiritual heroics; it's the result of Jesus's finished work. You can't get any cozier than being *in* Christ (1 Corinthians 15:22), nor can Jesus get any more "in you" than He already is (Colossians 1:27). This union with Him isn't some abstract theological idea—it's your daily reality.

And how do we gauge this closeness? By clocking in more Bible study hours, marathon prayer sessions, or racking up church attendance badges? Hardly. This isn't a feeling to chase but a fact to rest in, cemented by the blood of Jesus (Ephesians 2:14) and His resurrection, sealing our forever union with Him.

When Jesus prayed in John 17, He didn't whisper into the void:

> "that they may all be one; even as You, Father, are in Me and I in You, that they also may be in Us, so that the world may believe that You sent Me. The glory which You have given Me I have given to them, that they may be one, just as We are one; I in them and You in Me, that they may be perfected in unity, so that the world may know that You sent Me, and loved them, even as You have loved Me" (John 17:21–23)

His plea for our union with Him was answered. We're not inching closer to God with every religious step—we were catapulted into His presence by the cross and superglued into oneness by the resurrection. This isn't a fluctuating experience; it's an unbreakable bond.

Comparing our union with God to earthly relationships is like comparing galaxies and marbles. Sure, our understanding of His love grows, but let's not kid ourselves—no human analogy can fully capture the supernatural fusion of Christ in us. It required blood and resurrection, not warm fuzzies.

Maybe you've thought about quoting James in your quest for "getting closer" to God?

> Draw near to God and He will draw near to you. Cleanse your hands, you sinners; and purify your hearts, you double-minded. (James 4:8)

But that's for the undecided! (Note: That's why James calls them sinners, not saints.) Believers have already drawn near—we're seated at

God's right hand, perfectly fused with Jesus forever. Cleansing, purifying, unifying? We've already got all that in spades!

This isn't a ladder to climb but a gift to unwrap. It's not about your emotions—it's about the rock-solid fact of your oneness with Christ. Our journey isn't a hike toward God; it's a deep dive into the vastness of His love, with us firmly tethered to Him from start to finish.

Now, let's demystify "abiding" in Christ—a term some use like it's a spiritual marathon we need to train for. "Abiding" simply means living, and the moment you believed, you checked in for an eternal stay. It's not some conditional timeshare—it's your permanent residence.

And those branches that don't abide in John 15? They're *burned*. Yes, burned. So, if you think you're jumping in and out of "abiding" every twenty-seven minutes, ask yourself: Could I be burned if Jesus returned at an inconvenient moment? No. Jesus's command to abide was an invitation to live in Him forever, not a revolving door of fear.

And let's talk about "putting God first," like He's in a competition for your attention alongside your grocery list. Seriously? Christ isn't jockeying for first place—He is your life, the very air you breathe (Colossians 3:4). He's not another line item on your spiritual to-do list.

So, brothers and sisters, we're not on some endless quest to "get close" to God. We've been perfectly grafted into Him through Christ's work, not ours. Our journey is about renewing our minds to this truth, not chasing after something we've already got.

So shake off the false modesty and embrace your inheritance. You're not trespassing on God's glory by acknowledging your place in it—you're living out the reality of your rebirth. It's time to stop striving for something that's already yours.

Clean and close forever, just like you,
Andronicus and Johannes

SIZING UP HIS LOVE

To the Congregational Czars with Their Monotone Melodies:

We wish to address a doctrine so buried beneath the fog of modern religiosity that its true brilliance is as hidden as humility at a celebrity awards show: our unchangeable zip code in the Spirit.

Let's start with the scandalously ignored postcard from Paul in Romans 8:9, a message so overlooked it might as well have been written in invisible ink:

> However, you are not in the flesh but in the Spirit, if indeed the Spirit of God dwells in you. But if anyone does not have the Spirit of Christ, he does not belong to Him. (Romans 8:9)

Paul asserts, with all the subtlety of a sledgehammer, that we're not just weekend guests in the Spirit's house—we've moved in for good. Permanent residency: "In the Spirit" stamped on our spiritual passports.

Yet, judging by the spiritual schizophrenia running rampant in some teachings, you'd think we're in some cosmic game of musical chairs, constantly shifting between being "in the flesh" and "in the Spirit" based on how many hymns we've sung or whether we had a few unsavory thoughts at work.

Paul, with the enthusiasm of a toddler on Christmas morning, lays out the stark difference between a flesh-bound unbeliever and a Spirit-dwelling believer. Yet somehow, there's still a crowd peddling the idea that we hop between these two realms like undecided voters—depending on whether we gossiped about Sister Margaret's questionable casserole or tithed enough for the new building fund.

The New Testament writers, in a group effort, make it clear we've swapped our citizenship from the dominion of darkness to the kingdom of light faster than a politician changes talking points (Colossians 1:13 comes to mind). We've gone from spiritual couch potatoes to marathon runners in righteousness, though you wouldn't know it by the way we agonize over every slip-up like a teenager with their first pimple.

And yet, modern Christendom's obsession with legalistic hoop-jumping is as tragic as trying to bail out the Titanic with a teacup. We're so busy policing behavior, we've missed the point: living in the Spirit isn't about flawless performance—it's about aligning our perspective with who we already are in Christ.

When we make sin our pet project, it fits about as well as a piano in a minivan—not because we're failures, but because we're simply incompatible with sin. Like a penguin at a beach party, we just don't belong with sin. Our spiritual geography doesn't fluctuate based on performance; our permanent address is "in the Spirit"—even if we sometimes forget to forward our mail.

Now, let's address the idea of being "filled with the Spirit"—a term that's become more loaded than a baked potato at a steakhouse. The phrase has been bandied about, often equated with spiritual showmanship like speaking in tongues or bending spoons with your mind. But if you take a dive into Scripture, it's less about spiritual pyrotechnics and more about the day-to-day miracles of love, serving others, and enduring life's curveballs with grace.

Ephesians 5:18, with a hint of humor, juxtaposes getting sloshed on wine with being filled with the Spirit. The comparison is both amusing and profound: both influence behavior, but only one leads to singing from the heart, gratitude, and mutual submission—without the hangover.

Ephesians 3 takes it further: being filled with the Spirit is not about showcasing one's spiritual feats. It's about being so drenched in Christ's love that it spills out in our words, actions, and even our silence.

The invitation isn't to rack up a spiritual high score but to dive so deep into Christ's love that coming up for air seems ridiculous. Let's trade the fleeting rush of spiritual spectacle for the enduring embrace of a love that shapes our very being.

From the outskirts of conventional religiosity,
Andronicus and Johannes

GIFT SHIFT

To the Devout Disciples and the Tongue-Tied Travelers:

Buckle up—it's time for a candid chat. Today's headline: "Tongues and Prophecy—Why We Don't Need to Be Alarmed, Mystified, or Downright Freaked Out by These Gifts." After all, they're designed to build up the church, not scare us to death!

Let's dive into the drama, shall we? Tongues and prophecy have been misrepresented, misconstrued, and generally mangled by well-meaning folks who missed the memo. Some insist tongues are the ultimate badge to prove your salvation, while others are on a never-ending quest for the next spiritual high. Time to set the record straight.

First up: Prophecy, which 1 Corinthians 14:3 spells out crystal clear: Prophecy is for "edification, exhortation, and consolation." That's right, folks—it's about building up, inspiring, and comforting. Prophecy isn't your personal fortune teller predicting next week's lottery numbers or spilling divine secrets with a crystal ball. It's a loving reminder of Gospel truth applied to your life, for your good.

Let's also squash that prophecy is some wild, uncontrollable force. Paul makes it plain: "the spirits of prophets are subject to the control of prophets" (1 Corinthians 14:32). Translation? It's orderly, controlled, and always geared toward helping others.

Now, let's talk tongues. Acts 2:8 gives us the definitive rundown: tongues are about sharing the Gospel in a listener's native language. Think of it as the ultimate missionary tool—not some mystical, angelic babble, but real, understandable speech for evangelism.

In Acts 2, the apostles spoke in tongues to a diverse crowd, and each person heard the Gospel in their own language—then believed. This is the only example of "tongues" you'll find in Scripture. The takeaway? The gift of tongues is about communication, not confusion.

Some folks trip over Paul's mention of "tongues of angels" in 1 Corinthians 13, but it's hyperbole—Paul's way of stressing the importance of love. He also talked about moving mountains and getting burned at the stake (neither of which he did!). He wasn't claiming Luke Skywalker superpowers or some private angelic language!

And what about Jude 1:20's "praying in the Spirit"? It's just talking to God with full confidence in our perfect connection with Him. It's not about tongues at all—it's the only way to pray, every time, all the time. That's why Ephesians 6:18 says, "pray at all times in the Spirit."

God doesn't give special gifts or spiritual trinkets that signify a superior relationship with Him. He doesn't play that game. Spiritual gifts are for the benefit of *others*. A prayer language where we receive special insight, revelation, or our own personal "good vibes" just isn't in God's plan. Could we stop trying to out-spiritual each other, please?

So, to those convinced tongues are a private prayer language—sorry to burst your bubble. Tongues are for evangelism in real languages, not self-edification. Spiritual gifts exist to build up others (Ephesians 4:12), not to inflate ourselves. They're given by the Spirit, not taught in a classroom or mimicked in a prayer circle.

Some latch onto 1 Corinthians 14:2 to justify speaking secret mysteries to God in a private, spiritual code. But context is key! Paul is talking about church services, not your personal prayer closet. When he says, "For one who speaks in a tongue does not speak to men but to God; for no one understands, but in his spirit he speaks mysteries," he's not handing out gold stars. He's highlighting the problem—babbling in a foreign (human) language at church leaves everyone scratching their heads. Later, he compares it to sounding like a barbarian (1 Corinthians 14:11) and asks if outsiders will think you're off your rocker (1 Corinthians 14:23). His fix? Speak with your mind, ensuring your words benefit others. Cherry-picking 14:2 to validate a private prayer language yanks it out of context and misses Paul's plea for order in corporate worship.

In conclusion, we don't need a spiritual circus to feel close to God. We're already fully fitted into Him through Christ's work, not our own efforts. Our journey is about enjoying that closeness, not hunting it down. And for the skeptics, Paul's words in 1 Corinthians 14:22 say it all: "Tongues are a sign, not for believers but for unbelievers." Tongues are meant to reach those who haven't heard the Gospel yet, in a language they can understand. Let's stop turning spiritual gifts into a badge of honor or a sideshow act. Instead, let's focus on their true purpose—to glorify God and build up others.

We're called to embrace our spiritual inheritance, live out the truth of our unity with Christ, and quit chasing experiences. We're here to build up the church, spread the Gospel, and live in the boundless freedom of grace and truth.

Speaking in love (not tongues),
Andronicus and Johannes, advocates of clear-cut grace and no-nonsense spirituality

SIGNED, SEALED, DELIVERED

To the Spiritual Warfare Enthusiasts:

It seems we've stepped into an ecclesiastical episode of "Who Wants to Be a Demon Slayer?"—where every Tom, Dick, and Harry feels the need to exorcise demons like they're auditioning for prime-time TV. Let's get one thing straight: your primary calling isn't to land the lead in the next *Exorcist* sequel but to stand firm in the truth of who you are in Christ—holy, righteous, blameless, protected, and sealed by the Holy Spirit.

Now, let's talk turkey. The trend of majoring in demon-slaying while minoring in Gospel-preaching is like showing up to a battle with marshmallows instead of swords. You're putting on a spiritual warfare circus, but folks leave with more questions than answers: "How can I know I'm saved?" "Am I saved forever?" "Am I safe from the enemy?" "How do I set my mind?" "What's the truth here?" "How do I walk by the Spirit?" "Can I just ignore the enemy and focus on Jesus?"

Instead of feeding believers solid spiritual nourishment, we're dishing out cotton candy theology. It's sweet but leaves them undernourished. The truth is, you're safer in Christ than in any demon-centered combat class. God doesn't do timeshares with the enemy. Sure, we get tempted, accused, and afflicted, but let's settle this once and for all: believers are never owned by the enemy.

Yet here we are, staging cosmic drama productions where Satan gets more screen time than the Savior. The church seems more focused on demon dialogue than divine discourse. Yes, Satan's real, and yes, he's out for no good, but he doesn't need a spotlight or a grand campaign from us to do his dirty work.

Consider the armor of God—a concept some have twisted into a checklist of behavior rather than seeing it as the full embodiment of Christ. The belt of truth? *Jesus* is the Truth. The breastplate of righteousness? *Jesus* is our righteousness. Feet shod with the Gospel of peace? *Jesus* is the Prince of Peace. The helmet of salvation? *Jesus* is our salvation. The sword of the Spirit (the Word of God)? *Jesus* is the living Word!

And then there's the shield of faith—faith in whom? *Jesus Christ*, of course. This is how we stand against the enemy, not by upgrading our spiritual warfare strategy but by resting in the truth of who we already are in Him. We've already got everything we need for life and godliness (2 Peter 1:3–4).

Let's clear up a common myth: Satan doesn't have it out for you because you're doing something "big for God." He doesn't wake up one morning, put on his reading glasses, and think, "Oh no, Bob McGregor is about to lead a prayer group. Let's make him lose his wallet!" No, Satan wants bad things for all of us, all the time. He doesn't need a special reason. And God never says, "Oh no! I forgot about Bob! I wish someone was doing warfare prayers on his behalf. Now excuse Me, I've got to go find Bob's wallet."

Yes, God loves our prayers, and in ways beyond understanding, He chooses to work through them. But we don't need to teach people to yell at Satan or take "authority" over what we presume Satan's up to. And Bob's wallet? He probably misplaced it. Help him retrace his steps—no need to yell at Satan about it; he probably has no idea where it is either.

As for the spectacle of demon hunting under every bush of circumstance, it's time to drop the curtain. The ultimate answer to spiritual warfare, for believers and unbelievers, is the Gospel. Believers? We're God's possession—the evil one can't touch us (1 John 5:18). Unbelievers? Call on the name of the Lord and be saved—God cleans house and moves in. End of story.

Let's stop the theatrics and focus on what really matters: teaching people who they are in Christ. Arm them with the Gospel, not with dramatic declarations for their next demon duel. Equip them to stand firm in Christ's finished work—not in their own spiritual performances.

In the bulletproof protection of Jesus,
Andronicus and Johannes, Guardians of the Gospel (not Directors of Demons)

THE PROSPERITY PITFALL

To the Modern-Day Money-Changers and Their Vulnerable Victims:

We're here to call out a plague—one known as the health-wealth prosperity gospel. This poisonous doctrine whispers seductive promises of guaranteed riches and perfect health, like a spiritual Ponzi scheme. It lures the desperate with glittering hopes, only to leave them poorer, sicker, and utterly empty-handed.

But our sacred texts sing a different tune. The Apostle Paul, in his letter to the Philippians, reveals a secret far more precious than the fleeting charms of wealth or the mirage of perpetual health:

> I have learned to be content in whatever circumstances I am. I know how to get along with humble means, and I also know how to live in prosperity; in any and every circumstance I have learned the secret of being filled and going hungry, both of having abundance and suffering need. (Philippians 4:11b–12)

Paul speaks of a treasure that's immune to the ups and downs of fortune—contentment in Christ. Meanwhile, the prosperity gospel stands as a golden calf draped in a veneer of faith. It peddles a God who operates more like a slot machine than the sovereign Creator of the universe.

"Insert tithe, pull down the handle of faith, and out come your financial returns," it proclaims. But 1 Timothy 6 slaps down this lie, declaring that godliness with contentment is great gain and rebuking those who treat godliness as a get-rich scheme. Paul labels them as "men of depraved mind and deprived of the truth, who suppose that godliness is a means of gain" (1 Timothy 6:5).

Paul's own life was no parade of prosperity—his journey was a testament to relying on Christ in the face of hunger, need, and suffering. His epistles, inconveniently for prosperity preachers, outline a life rich in spiritual abundance, even while materially lacking.

This warped gospel not only misrepresents God's blessing as a fat bank account but also dangerously implies that illness is a sign of spiritual failure. Yet, the New Testament is littered with examples of faithful servants—Paul with his thorn, Timothy with his stomach issues—whose ailments didn't reflect a lack of faith but the harsh realities of a broken world. Paul's thorn serves as a reminder that our strength is found in Christ, not in perfect health.

Let's be real: if the health-wealth gospel were true, then the apostles were the biggest spiritual flops in history. Where was Peter's private jet? Where was John's mansion on the Mediterranean? These men, who walked closest with Jesus, faced prison, beatings, and martyrdom. They were rich in faith, not in material wealth. If we follow the prosperity gospel logic, we'd have to believe Paul's shipwrecks were divine hints that he hadn't "claimed" enough blessings.

And then there's Job, the poster child for righteous suffering. He lost everything despite his unwavering faith. His story alone shatters the idea that financial or physical suffering is a sign of weak faith. God Himself praised Job's faithfulness, even in the pit of misery. So let's ask: if faith were a guarantee of health and wealth, why would God allow His most faithful servants to endure such hardships?

> And He has said to me, "My grace is sufficient for you, for power is perfected in weakness. Most gladly, therefore, I will rather boast about my weaknesses, so that the power of Christ may dwell in me." (2 Corinthians 12:9)

The allure of the prosperity gospel is understandable—who wouldn't want a guarantee of health and wealth? But Jesus warned us about the trials and hatred we'd face in this world, not a fast track to financial success (John 16:33; Matthew 10:22). This road we're called to walk isn't paved with gold but with the solid promises of Christ. Meanwhile, the health-wealth gospel tries to reroute believers onto a boulevard of broken dreams.

The real Gospel offers a prosperity that isn't measured by bank statements or medical charts but by the riches of knowing Christ. Jesus Himself asked:

> "For what will it profit a man if he gains the whole world and forfeits his soul?" (Matthew 16:26)

The obsession with wealth and health distracts from the Gospel's true promise: a relationship with Christ and the eternal security He brings. If financial wealth were the hallmark of God's favor, Jesus would've lived in a palace, not as a poor carpenter who died a brutal death.

Moreover, the health-wealth gospel perpetuates a cruel lie—that poverty or illness is evidence of a lack of faith. This cheap ideology dismisses the trials that many believers face, robbing them of the comfort found in God's promises. James writes:

> Consider it all joy, my brethren, when you encounter various trials, knowing that the testing of your faith produces endurance. (James 1:2–3)

These trials aren't a sign of God's disfavor—they're opportunities to grow in faith and lean on Him. The shallow promises of prosperity preaching pale in comparison to the deep spiritual maturity and contentment found in Christ alone.

As we expose the falsehoods of the health-wealth gospel, let's remember the true riches of the Kingdom. Our prosperity isn't counted in dollars or perfect health, but in the boundless grace and eternal security offered by Christ. Let's shun the snake oil and cling to the true Gospel—where our sufficiency is in Christ, not in the fleeting, fickle promises of the world.

In a world obsessed with the external, let's ground our faith in the internal, eternal truths of Scripture. The health-wealth gospel peddles a shortcut, but the true Gospel provides a path to lasting peace, true fulfillment, and unshakeable joy in Christ.

A toast to the secret of contentment—Jesus Himself,
Andronicus and Johannes

PERFECTION PARANOIA

To the Navigators of the Divine Maze:

Let's stop tiptoeing around the misguided obsession with "finding God's will" and then trying to "stay in it"—just another flavor of the prosperity gospel, with cushy circumstances replacing cold, hard cash. This frantic pursuit of hidden messages, promising a life free from hardship to those who crack the code, is nothing short of spiritual quackery. It promises that with enough faith, enough listening for secret messages, and enough right choices, you unlock the "prosperity" of better circumstances and outcomes. The wake it leaves behind? Disillusioned believers with sky-high expectations and deep disappointment with a God who didn't shield them from life's tough knocks.

Let's cut to the chase: the idea that God's will is some tightrope we have to gingerly tiptoe across, lest we plunge into the abyss of His displeasure, is not only exhausting—it's unbiblical. It's as if we've reimagined the Almighty as a divine chess master, maneuvering us like pawns, and each decision must be perfect, or the whole game collapses. But here's the thing—God's will isn't a riddle we have to solve before the buzzer goes off.

Romans 12:2 doesn't tell us to decode some heavenly message. It exhorts us to be transformed by renewing our minds, so we can discern what God's will is—what's good, acceptable and perfect. It's not a scavenger hunt (what house, what spouse, what car, what cereal). It's a life lived in reliance on Christ's power. In short, God's will is Jesus Himself—alive in you and expressing Himself through you. Paul doesn't present God's will as a game of spiritual Sudoku but a call to know Christ, express Him, and be transformed by His life within.

Now, let's dig deeper. What if God's will isn't about where we go or what we do, but who we reflect as we go and do? Maybe it's not about which job we take but how we love others in that job. Not about what house we buy, but about how we love others in that home. It's almost like God is more interested in the fruit of the Spirit (Galatians 5:22–23) showing up in our lives than in our five-year strategic plan.

As 1 Timothy 2:4 and 2 Peter 3:9 tell us, God's will (His desire) is for all to come to repentance and know the truth—not to navigate some elaborate obstacle course of cryptic choices. Even Paul, with all his missionary zeal, admitted his plans got derailed more than once (Romans 1:13). Paul packed his bags for Rome several times and had to unpack them again. Apparently, he wasn't equipped with a secret decoder ring for flawless decisions and perfect outcomes.

Let's get even more real: the obsession with "finding God's will" masquerades as a holy pursuit, but it's often a thinly veiled desire to dodge discomfort. We've swallowed the lie that God's will leads to comfort and success, and anything less means we've messed up. But we forget that the Spirit led Jesus into the wilderness to be tempted

(Matthew 4:1), and God's will led Him to the cross—not exactly a cushy path. If God's will led the sinless Savior to suffering, what makes us think we're entitled to a life of uninterrupted bliss?

And here's the elephant in the room: fear. Fear of making the wrong choice. Fear of stepping outside of God's "perfect" plan. Fear of the unknown. But here's the truth that sets you free: God isn't perched on His throne with a giant red marker, waiting to grade every choice as right or wrong. The real problem isn't a lack of divine breadcrumbs leading us to prosperity but a famine of understanding about the riches of a life lived in union with Christ.

Let's not overlook the irony here. While we're agonizing over decisions, trying to crack the code of God's will, we often miss what He's clearly revealed. Love others as He has loved us. Forgive as we've been forgiven. Walk by the Spirit. These aren't riddles or cryptic messages—they're the plain, crystal-clear instructions from a loving Father. It's almost as if we've become so obsessed with mystery that we've forgotten the simplicity of living out our faith in the ordinary, everyday moments of life.

It's time for the church to cast aside the chains of morbid theology and the paralyzing quest for "God's will." Let's instead embrace the freedom of simply living by faith in Christ's sufficiency. God's will isn't a tightrope—it's a playground. We're free to explore, create, and enjoy life within the wide-open spaces of His grace. He's given us His Spirit to guide us, His Word to instruct us, and the freedom to make choices without the fear of missing some elusive, hidden target. The sooner we stop hunting for the X that marks the spot, and start enjoying the treasure we already have in Jesus, the sooner we'll experience the joy and freedom of truly living in God's will—living in Christ!

So, let's drop the act. God's will isn't a cosmic puzzle. It's not divine hide-and-seek where we hope to stumble upon the right answer. It's Jesus—plain and simple. When we rest in Him, trust in His finished work, and express the life He's given us, we're not just in God's will—we're thriving in it.

With you, right at the center of God's will,
Andronicus and Johannes

PARTY GOSPEL?

To the Politically Entangled and the Heavenly Citizens:

Let's talk about an entanglement that's snagging many well-meaning believers these days—the sticky web of politics and faith.

Remember, Jesus lived during intense political turmoil under Roman rule. Yet, He didn't launch a political reform campaign or seek to overthrow the Roman government. His mission? Clear and profound: to establish a kingdom not of this world. Likewise, the Apostle Paul crisscrossed the Greek world preaching the Gospel of a heavenly citizenship (Philippians 3:20), not a government overhaul. Neither of them signed up for the political circus of their time.

Now, let's be clear: engaging in politics isn't the issue. Absolutely, vote, advocate, be good citizens. But let's not mistake our faith for a political platform. Some of us have been sold the lie that true Christianity requires perfect alignment with a specific ideology. This can divert us from our real mission and send a confusing message to the world.

Sure, government matters. God's all for it—Romans 13:1 shows us He endorses leadership to maintain order. It's how the buses run on time, the mail gets delivered, and trash is picked up—so God doesn't have to part the heavens every time someone loses a shed in a tornado.

But let's not kid ourselves—political power is a seductive beast. It whispers the illusion of control, of bending the world to our righteous vision. But remember, the Gospel isn't about control; it's about submitting to Another. When we forget that, we risk turning our political victories into idols and our defeats into crises of faith. The Gospel calls us higher—to a peace that transcends winning or losing at the ballot box and a kingdom that can't be rattled by political turmoil.

No earthly government shares the same goals as the Gospel. Let's face it: every political party has some agenda that would make Jesus say, "Yeah, I'm not lobbying for that" (whether it's riding an elephant or a donkey). The straw man of the political Jesus divides us from our neighbors and from conversations that offer the real Jesus—the one who transcends party lines and policies.

So, let's not reduce the Gospel to a set of talking points. It's like trying to stuff the infinite power of the resurrection into a voting booth. It doesn't work. Christianity is about a transformative relationship with Christ, not about ticking off political boxes.

The Gospel has been around for millennia, outlasting every nation, every political system. With that kind of historical context, it's easy to see: Christianity is not a political party. It's not red, blue, or any shade in between. Our identity in Christ runs deeper than any political allegiance. It's deeper than being a conservative or liberal. Deeper than our national identity. We are citizens of Heaven, and that shapes us far more than any earthly party line.

Yes, vote with passion, care deeply, and engage thoughtfully. But maybe skip the part where we shout that one party is God's party and the other is the citadel of Satan. Instead, let's practice loving those who fiercely disagree with us—without necessarily agreeing with them. This builds bridges across political divides and shifts the conversation to the heart of the matter: Who is Jesus, and what did He come to do for us?

And let's not overlook the lurking danger of self-righteousness that can creep in when we equate our political stance with spiritual purity. The Pharisees thought they were on the right side of every issue and yet missed the Messiah standing right in front of them. We must guard against the temptation to become gatekeepers of divine truth based on our political leanings. True righteousness is found in Christ alone, not in our ability to win a political argument. Our mission is to reflect His grace, not our moral superiority.

Don't reduce Christianity to a checklist of policies. You can't legislate love; it's the fruit of the Spirit (Galatians 5:22–23). And the Gospel calls us to a higher allegiance—one that transcends political boundaries and national identities. Political agendas come and go, but the message of Christ endures forever.

With eyes on the eternal,
Andronicus and Johannes

PART 5

NEW-SELF SYMPHONY

SHARED FATE

To the Sermon Soldiers and Their Distressed Disciples:

Greetings and salutations! Today, we embark on a journey through the tale of two identities: the one you've been sold and the one you've been made into in Christ. Why the discrepancy? Well, it boils down to this: the finished work of Jesus doesn't just drag us to a funeral for our sins—it invites us to the ultimate birthday bash for our new selves.

According to the Apostle Paul, you're dead! And no, not in the "wear black and play a sad violin" kind of way, but in the "crucified with Christ" sense of Galatians 2:20 and Romans 6:6. This isn't your run-of-the-mill obituary; it's a once-in-forever event where you check out of Motel Sin and check into the five-star Ritz of Righteousness. You're free from the tyranny of do's and don'ts that haunt the halls of modern Christianity. So why are so many of us playing ghost, haunting our own lives with chains of "Do not handle, do not taste, do not touch!" (Colossians 2:20–21)? Spooky stuff indeed.

Ah, the siren song of legalism—there's nothing quite like a good old list of rules to give your heart a jolt, right? Wrong. Somewhere along the line, we've confused the glorious symphony of salvation with a cacophony of commandments, as if the Gospel were a home improvement project. But here's the kicker: Jesus didn't take the plunge into death just to give us a moral makeover. He pulled us up into a new creation reality (2 Corinthians 5:17). We're not Frankenstein's monster, patched together with scraps of good deeds and religious rituals. We're divinely designed, pre-approved, and delivered straight from the domain of darkness into the Kingdom of Light.

In Romans 6, Paul asks what's on everyone's mind, "If we're dead to sin and alive to God, why are we acting like spiritual zombies?" Good question, Paul. It's as if we've mistaken the Gospel for a ghost story, where we spend our days battling our ghoulish old selves. But the truth? Our old self is as dead as disco. Gone, kaput, finito—like every mafia kingpin you've ever heard of. And in its place? A shiny, new, sin-resistant self that's ready to live out its divine destiny. And no, this isn't just theological jargon—it's a reality check issued from The Bank of Zion.

So, why the long faces and the longer list of rules? Maybe we've been so busy trying to tame our supposedly sinister selves that we missed the memo on our miraculous makeup? The truth is, this identity crisis isn't a personal failure—it's a masterclass in deception by the enemy. A believer unaware of their true identity is like a lion living on tofu—full of potential but painfully malnourished.

Look, living this new life isn't about becoming a poster child for piety. It's about embracing your Christ-infused identity and letting that truth inspire everything you do. As James so eloquently put it, doers of the Word are people who look in the mirror, see who they really are, walk away, and remember what they look like.

So, dear brethren, here's the truth: We've been co-resurrected with Christ. This isn't just theology—it's your new reality. Think of the Gospel as the ultimate coming-of-age story, where we're not the problem, we're the heroes of God's redemptive plot.

Living in the reality of the resurrection,
Andronicus and Johannes

THE EMULSIFIER

To the Theologians Who Have No Clothes and Those Who Only Think They're Naked:

Many of us have been cast in a tragic film titled *The Enduring Sinner*. It's a real tearjerker, filled with the highs of temptation and the lows of transgression. In this sad tale, our heroes (yep, that's us) struggle against their worst enemy—who, inconveniently, looks back at them from the mirror.

But let's be real: this script is more outdated than a floppy disk at a tech conference. Romans 6 doesn't hedge its bets; it flat-out tells us we're "dead to sin but alive to God in Christ Jesus." Not dead-ish, not alive-ish. No, it's a full-on, irrevocable upgrade—out with the old, in with the brand-new.

Now, let's address this "saved sinner" narrative we keep dragging around like a bad sequel. If we keep casting ourselves as the divine disappointment, we're not just selling ourselves short; we're buying into a bargain bin theology where grace is a clearance item, not the premium product it truly is.

Enter the emulsifier—our sacred catalyst. It doesn't just clean up our act; it changes the very fabric of our being. Just like an egg binds oil and vinegar into a harmonious whole, Christ binds our mortal mess with His divine DNA. Our identity isn't just refurbished; it's reborn. The old labels? Expired. The new tag? "Alive in Christ."

The emulsifier—yes, that golden yolk of divine intervention—has whisked together our oil-and-water existence into a heavenly blend of sanctified serenity. We're not just spicing up some bland theology here—no, we've been remade. In Christ, our very essence is transformed, making the mix not just palatable but perfect. Where once we were a separated, lumpy mess, we're now a smooth, inseparable masterpiece—crafted by the Ultimate Chef.

Here's the bottom line: We are not what we do. We are who He declares us to be. Our past, present, and future sins? Forgiven. Our identity? Sealed in the sacred synergy of our union with Christ. This isn't a temporary makeover; it's an eternal, irreversible transformation. We've gone from sin-soaked wanderers to sanctified wonders.

And yet, here we are, still trying to fit into the outdated, itchy garments of "must-try-harder" and "not-good-enough," forgetting that in the grand ballroom of grace, those outfits are so last century. The truth is, we've been handed robes of righteousness—not as rentals but as gifts, eternal and irrevocable. In this walk-in closet of wonder, there's no room for the moth-eaten threads of guilt or the tattered rags of self-effort. Only the finest attire, woven from the fabric of grace, go perfectly with the resurrection righteousness we carry on the inside.

The Gospel isn't a gauntlet of guilt but a gala of grace. So don't mope in the mire of "might-have-beens" but march in the majesty of who you now are—knowing Jesus is your everything. Go ahead, maybe even strut like it.

Never a wardrobe malfunction,
Andronicus and Johannes

MORBID MESSAGES

To the Overseers of Orthodoxy and Those Anchored in Anguish:

In our noble quest for piety, we seem to have wandered off the well-trodden path into the wilderness of Scriptural misinterpretation, convinced that "dying daily" (1 Corinthians 15:30–32) and taking up our cross daily (Luke 9:23) are holy mandates for a soul-crushing, joy-stealing version of spiritual self-flagellation.

Let's set the record straight: when Paul talked about facing death daily, he wasn't setting up a spiritual boot camp. He was talking about dodging actual death threats—like when wild beasts were coming for him near Ephesus (and no, that wasn't a metaphor for an angry church board). As for carrying our cross? It's not a daily drag of self-denial but a one-time deal, embracing our death to sin's power and our resurrection to a radical new life in God.

Now let's untangle the mess that's been made out of the "flesh" (Greek: *sarx*). Somehow, we've twisted it into this mythical "sinful nature" that we're supposed to purge daily like bad toxins from a juice cleanse. Newsflash: the New Testament's mention of flesh isn't some dark admission of dual citizenship in God's kingdom and the realm of inherent wickedness. No, it's more like old, buggy software (thought patterns) clashing with our shiny, new heartware (new self). Remember, you really are different at the core:

- "if anyone is in Christ, he is a new creature" (2 Corinthians 5:17)
- "you laid aside the old self with its evil practices" (Colossians 3:9)
- "[you] have put on the new self who is being renewed to a true knowledge" (Colossians 3:9)
- "you became obedient from the heart" (Romans 6:17)
- "you became slaves of righteousness" (Romans 6:18)

Now, let's address the elephant in the sanctuary: the misapplication of Jesus's challenge to "hate one's life" and the call to self-denial (John 12:25; Matthew 16:24–26). Jesus wasn't handing out lifetime memberships to the Self-Loathing Club. He was talking about entering into a radical, life-transforming union with Him. Sign the dotted line once, and you're in. You hate your old life, so you follow Jesus into death, and boom—you're reborn. Simple, right?

Paul's past-tense party in Galatians 2:20 and Romans 6:6 about being crucified with Christ wasn't an open invitation to daily reenactments of our own crucifixion. No need to call Mel Gibson to direct or anything. It's a done deal. The old you? Gone. The new you? Alive and kicking here and now.

For those who've turned "dying to self" into a daily grind, you've missed the mark. This isn't a divine directive (no, the phrase is literally nonexistent within the Good Book). It's a tragic case of theological telephone gone horribly wrong. The Scriptures shout it from the rooftops: your old self was nailed to the cross once and for all (Romans 6:3–4). This isn't about embracing a spiritual death wish; it's about living in the victory of Jesus's resurrection. Stop trying to die to self—you *are* the new self. Why try to kill what God has already made new?

The perpetual self-denial narrative is like a broken record—except it's not music to anyone's ears. It's a gloomy gospel of self-sabotage, missing the point of Jesus's finished work on the cross. Friends, we're not called to be spiritual zombie-martyrs, wandering the earth in a state of constant self-denial. Our identity is not a "dead man walking" but a brand-new creation. Alive to God, we're living a life that's more Technicolor Dreamcoat than sackcloth and ashes (2 Corinthians 5:17).

So, how about we ditch the self-destruction and embrace the vibrant celebration of our new self in Jesus Christ? Our daily agenda isn't to die—it's to live. Don't deny yourself if you're the new self. Be yourself. Go ahead, swap the morbidity of self-denial for the beauty of a life fully alive in Him, putting the fruit of the Spirit on display in full HD.

Yes, the Gospel really is this good. You can be yourself and express Jesus at the same time. You're not an obstacle to God—you're His instrument.

God is smiling right at you, and so are we,
Andronicus and Johannes

YOUR RIGHTEOUS REALITY

To the Gospel Gatekeepers and Their Youth Yoked by Yesteryear:

Here's one that's tickled the brains of church fathers, mothers, and distant relatives for centuries: Is our righteousness a divine accounting trick or a genuine transformation at the core of our being?

Really, it's both. Yes, Paul went full CPA in Romans, emphasizing that "Abraham believed God, and it was *credited* to him as righteousness" (Romans 4:3). A divine ledger entry if there ever was one! But before you think your righteousness is just some celestial number-crunching, there's more to the story.

Galatians throws us a theological curveball—righteousness isn't just penciled in, it's poured into us at salvation. Like fresh-brewed coffee straight into your spirit:

> For if a law had been given that was able to impart life, then righteousness would indeed have been based on law. (Galatians 3:21b)

The Law could not impart life to make us righteous, but that's exactly what Jesus did: He injected life within us to make us righteous. That's why Romans 4:25 says Jesus was "raised for our justification." This isn't some bookkeeping formality; we're "resurrection righteous"—a real, tangible, life-infused righteousness. No smoke, no mirrors—just hardcore holiness.

Now, let's chew on this whole "born again" thing, shall we? It's not a tagline for a spiritual self-help book but the real McCoy of our new life in Jesus (see John 3). We've got his DNA running through us, making us genuinely righteous, not just dressed up in our Sunday best. Think about it: If God's our spiritual Father, then by golly, we're righteous through and through. John is right here to back this up, saying righteousness is our new normal—it's in our spiritual bloodline. In fact, John goes next level, daring to say we're as righteous as Jesus!

> the one who practices righteousness is righteous, just as He is righteous (1 John 3:7b)

Paul, always the dramatic, talks about our career change from sin seekers to righteousness addicts. We're "slaves of righteousness" (Romans 6:18). No metaphor here—it's who we are now. Have you ever felt more like a sin intern than a righteousness mogul? Paul would say, "Feelings, schmeelings—your new propensity is a spiritual fact, plain and simple." Our union with Christ's death and resurrection isn't just for Bible trivia night; it can rock our world:

> How shall we who died to sin still live in it? (Romans 6:2b)

We're not just sin's ex—we've remarried into righteousness. And for reasons as bizarre as pineapple on pizza, this mind-blowing truth gets shoved to the back pew. It's not theological fluff; it's the bedrock of our identity. Once we embrace our righteousness, we shed those ill-fitting old clothes of sin like last year's fashion disaster.

Don't settle for salvation's CliffsNotes. Our righteousness isn't some holy optical illusion where God squints at us through Christ-colored lenses. It's about being reborn into a righteousness that's as legit as our old sin game was strong. Righteousness is the very substance of our new selves. It's the heart of how we see ourselves, rock our relationship with God, and do life on Earth.

Now, there's lots of Sunday chatter reducing this righteousness to spiritual window dressing. Some folks even cling to Paul's "chief of sinners" line in 1 Timothy 1:15 like it's a lifetime label. But that's Paul glancing in the rearview mirror, not narrating his current status. Think of it this way: Jack Nicklaus might say he's the "chief of golfers," but he no longer competes on the PGA Tour anymore. Same with Paul—he was simply spotlighting his promotion from chief sinner to chief saint. That's a miracle available to us all.

It's time to toss out any theology that's got us chasing righteousness like a pot of gold at the end of a rainbow. We're not hunting for it; we're living and breathing it right now. Our daily grind isn't about becoming righteous—it's about expressing the righteousness that's woven into our very being. So, let's live boldly, unapologetically righteous—not as spiritual peacocks, but as walking, talking billboards of Christ's resurrection power.

Here's looking at you, and guess what? We like what we see.
Andronicus and Johannes

EMBRACED, NOT ERASED

To the Keepers of the Code and the Grieving Guests at Grace's Gate:

Bravo! You've managed to turn the Christian life into a never-ending game of dress-up. With Ephesians 4 as your fuel, you preach "put off the old self" and "put on the new self" like it's a daily wardrobe change. You're confusing the one-time, profound exchange for a daily chore.

Let's get technical. In Ephesians 4, Paul uses infinitive verbs (*to put off, to put on*), referring to what they were taught when they first heard the Gospel. They were taught that faith in Christ would involve becoming a whole new person. Paul never meant to inspire spiritual personality swaps on a daily basis. Colossians 3:10 spells it out even clearer: "have put on the new self." Why? Because it already happened at salvation! You have put off your old self and have put on your new self—no going back!

And let's not forget the much-loved misinterpretation of John the Baptist's "He must increase, but I must decrease" (John 3:30). You've turned this into a spiritual slimming program, totally missing John's actual point about the changing of the guard from his ministry to Jesus's. John wasn't suggesting we shrink our spiritual selves to fit into God's master plan. He was simply marking the handover from the warm-up act (his own ministry) to the main attraction (Jesus's ministry).

Now, here's another blunder. In Galatians 5:17, Paul says the flesh and the Spirit "are in opposition to one another, so that you may not do the things that you please." You really think sin pleases you? And the Holy Spirit is keeping you from it? That's a backwards interpretation that pits you against God's Spirit in a cosmic tug-of-war! In reality, it's the flesh that prevents you from the godly living that pleases you. Bottom line: You're on God's team!

Speaking of "teams," let's address the all-too-popular sentiment of "More of Him, less of me." This one sounds humble, but it's completely off-base. God isn't some divine minimalist, looking to declutter you from His eternal plans. He doesn't want "less of you" as if you're some inconvenience. It's not a question of reducing you; it's about infusing you with His life. He wants to embrace you, not erase you!

And that whole sculpting narrative? The idea that God is constantly chiseling away at us until nothing remains but His reflection? Let's dial it back a bit. God isn't running a demolition crew, knocking down everything about you until you disappear. He's more like a fire that illuminates without consuming—like the burning bush or at Pentecost. His presence doesn't obliterate you; it enhances you.

Now, about this "brokenness" obsession—you've turned growth into some kind of spiritual masochism. But here's the reality: You were broken before Christ, and now you're whole. Stop treating the Gospel like it's a self-destruction manual. Your new identity in Christ is about living fully, not about being shattered in a thousand pieces every day. God's work in you isn't about constantly breaking and remaking—you're already whole, already complete in Him.

And finally, let's talk about humility. You've painted a picture of God humbling us at every turn, but Scripture tells a different story. Humility is something we choose, not something God bulldozes us into. He's not forcing you down into the dust. He's inviting you to humble yourself. James and Peter are crystal clear on this:

- "humble yourselves" (James 4:10)
- "humble yourselves" (1 Peter 5:6)

The bottom line? You've been preaching a version of Christianity that's all about erasing the self, when the Gospel is about discovering who we truly are in Jesus Christ. Our unique new selves are not to be obliterated in God's presence. No, we are to shine brightly.

Here's the revolutionary truth: You can be yourself and express Jesus at the same time—no conflict, no tension, no contradiction. You're not an obstacle to God. You're His instrument, crafted for good works and filled with His life.

Realizing you're on God's team? It changes everything. Those thoughts, those desires, the deep longings of your heart? They're not something to fear or scrutinize—they're the very canvas upon which God is painting His masterpiece. Being yourself is the most authentic way to express Christ. You're not here to shrink. You're here to soar—boldly, fully, and gloriously alive in Him.

All of Him and all of us, in this beautiful, seamless union,
Andronicus and Johannes (indwelled, not expelled)

DIVINE ALGEBRA

To the Unshackled Souls and Enlightened Travelers on the Path Less Traveled:

By now you've hopefully cracked the code that the treasure we're all chasing is not buried on some far-off island but gleaming right inside us, shining in the "Sonlight" of revelation.

Yes, we get it. The whole "dying to self" thing has a certain poetic flair. It pirouettes on the lips of the devout with the elegance of a ballet dancer, yet trips over the tangled reality of a botched doctrine. It whispers sweet nothings of martyrdom, of a pious purging that seems so noble, so utterly devoted. But pause for a second: Is it not a little odd that we, the resurrected ones, citizens of a brand-new kingdom, are so obsessed with spiritually offing ourselves every day?

Here's the real kicker—the bizarre idea that our new, resurrected self is somehow a sneaky villain plotting our downfall. But how can that be when "Christ in us" is the very source of our new identity? Chasing the death of the self is like chasing your own shadow—it vanishes the moment you turn around and face reality.

The human penchant for proving devotion through suffering—how quaint! Yet Paul, with the finesse of a world-class debater, completely dismantles this notion. No amount of self-inflicted pain can add to the completeness of Christ's finished work. (Take a moment to enjoy Colossians 2:20–23 for this delightful truth.)

Ever seen that elusive manual on how to achieve self-mortification? Well, it doesn't exist, at least in God's library. Our journey isn't some step-by-step guide to spiritual annihilation; it's about embracing the fullness of our brand-new, shiny life in Christ.

But, hypothetically, let's say you managed to succeed in this bizarre ritual of self-execution every day. What then? Do you play a weird game of "whack-a-mole" with your resurrecting self, *ad infinitum*? Sounds exhausting, not to mention absurd.

Yes, the obsession with "dying to self" as a requirement for spiritual growth has ensnared many. It implies that every waking moment should be a litany of self-renunciation. But don't let this fallacy trip you up. Scripture sings a different tune—a melody of death leading to life, once and for all. The old self? Crucified with Christ. What's left? Not a menace to be exorcised but a life to be lived in the power of Jesus's resurrection.

Let's not twist the truth into a dreary doctrine of daily drudgery. Jesus didn't invite us to a life of constant spiritual suicide, but to a singular moment of radical truth—where we died with Him once and now live in the power of His resurrection forever. This isn't a daily dirge, folks; it's a call to freedom.

Think of it this way: In this divine romance, there's no surrender, because there is no battle with God. Our relationship with Him is not a contest of wills but a union of hearts, a harmonious alignment of desires. We are not vanquished foes but beloved partners, dancing in rhythm with His Spirit. In the heavenly equation, it's not about subtraction but multiplication. Christ in us doesn't diminish our essence but amplifies it.

Let us walk in the freedom of the Spirit, not marked by daily deaths but by new, eternal life. Our journey isn't about becoming less but realizing we are so much more in Him. It is not a path of self-erasure but self-discovery, where each step reveals more beauty—Christ in us and us in Christ.

Compatible with Christ,
Andronicus and Johannes, being ourselves (not denying ourselves)

HEART ATTACK

To the Connoisseurs of Completeness:

Let's finally settle that nagging question you've been dodging ever since you first squinted into your own spiritual mirror. Are we "just sinners saved by grace," doomed to shuffle around in guilt and shame, praying our spiritual Janitor—Jesus—can keep up with our endless mess? Or—brace yourself—are we actually something . . . good?

The "I'm a dirty sinner, but forgiven" anthem is catchy, sure. It's the sort of self-deprecating humility that pairs well with Christian bumper stickers and fridge magnets. We slap it on like a badge of honor, proudly shouting, "I'm not perfect, just forgiven!" But, seriously—is this really the hill Jesus died on? Is this the *big news* of the Gospel?

Breaking news! The Gospel isn't about making you feel perpetually unworthy. It's about declaring you brand-new. Sure, we all have a messy past, but it's God's performance, not ours, that perfects us.

This whole "dirty worm" theology—the idea that our hearts are deceitful above all else and desperately wicked—has held us in a chokehold for too long. We've been taught to distrust our hearts, to scrutinize every motive, and to fear the hidden closets within. It's like we're stuck in a spiritual haunted house, always waiting for the next skeleton to pop out and scream, "Gotcha! You're still a mess!"

But if you're in Christ, your heart isn't some haunted mansion with creaky floors and lurking ghosts. It's a holy sanctuary. God didn't perform a half-hearted renovation. He didn't just slap a "Jesus" label on your old, busted-up self and call it good. No, He performed a full-scale heart transplant. He gave you a new heart—one that's pure, obedient, and intrinsically good. Romans 6:17 celebrates this!

The endless routine of "examining" and "testing" our hearts? Exhausting. We're not spiritual lab rats constantly being poked and prodded. You've been given a heart that actually wants what God wants. It's trustworthy because it's His handiwork, not some beat-up fixer-upper on the brink of collapse.

Once you grasp this new-hearted identity, it changes everything—including how you handle failure and sin. Instead of falling into despair or self-condemnation, you recognize these moments are not a reflection of your true nature. You see them as opportunities to realign your thinking with your true self. Failure is not your identity—it's just bad acting.

The whole idea that your heart is a cesspool needing constant purification? That's a one-way ticket down a path of endless striving. But here's the truth bomb: If your new-hearted self is from God, it's fundamentally good. So why are we all so busy trying to prove otherwise?

Your desires, your spiritual instincts, your very core are good. You're not are war with yourself. You're simply learning to live from your new identity. Does this mean you'll never screw up? Of course not. But when you do, it's out of character—like showing up to a black-tie event in pajamas. Your real nature aligns with God's. You want what He wants.

Remember when Jesus talked about trees and their fruit? He said, "A good tree cannot bear bad fruit, and a bad tree cannot bear good fruit" (Luke 6:43). You're a good tree. You're designed for good works. Wired for a purpose. Your heart is good, your desires are pure, and your actions can flow from this divine wellspring.

Once this truth clicks, the striving stops. You don't need to fake love or manufacture forgiveness. It's who you are! A child of the resurrection with an obedient heart wired for good works. You don't need to be guilted into loving others—it's your nature. You forgive because it's what you do.

And really, what kind of cruel joke would it be for God to command you to "live good" if you were still bad inside. You'd never stand a chance! So, let's shed the old religious labels with their false humility and embrace our new reality in Christ. You are good. You are righteous. You are perfectly crafted for the life God has called you to live.

In the pure and perfect love of Christ,
Andronicus and Johannes

NEW HEART, NEW HORIZONS

To the Deep Thinkers and Heart-Seekers:

We've all heard the classic line: "I've got it all up here in my head. I just need to get it down here in my heart." Poetic, right? Not even close. That's like trying to perform brain surgery with a butter knife. We don't have it all sorted out upstairs. Our minds are in slow-mo renewal mode. The real treasure? That's in the heart.

When you joined Team Jesus, you didn't just get a moral touch-up; you got a full-blown heart transplant. That old, deceitful ticker? Gone. In its place—brand-new heartware. This wasn't a half-hearted renovation; it was a divine overhaul with zero shortcuts. So, next time someone tells you they've got it in their head but not in their heart, just smile and wave. True wisdom? It's already camping out in your heart where Jesus has set up headquarters.

Let's talk about the enemy's latest con job. He's pulled a fast one, convincing half the Christian population that their hearts are still "deceitfully wicked." And somehow, we've swallowed this lie, thinking it's the humble thing to do. But real humility? It's agreeing with

God about who we actually are. Want to know if your heart's still rotten or shiny and new? Ask the One who gave it to you.

Preachers of doom, you've been keeping folks in bondage, convincing them their hearts are still wicked. Your favorite go-to? Jeremiah 17:9: "The heart is more deceitful than all else, and is desperately sick." So, what do people do? They beat themselves up, repent more than they rejoice, and doubt their every motive.

Well, whatever a gig is, it's up. God is freeing your frightened followers, blowing the lid off your house of cards. You've fostered a weary, broken-hearted community of spiritual hypochondriacs who are popping antacids like candy. Guess what? They died, were raised in Christ, and got brand-new, God-filled hearts. A God-filled heart. No more deceit. Imagine if folks get their hands on this truth—more than a few religious authorities will be scrambling to write new sermons.

Can you trust your heart? Don't let your past screw-ups fool you. Hebrews 4:12 reminds us that God's Word is the only legit judge of our heart's intentions. It shines a spotlight on what's really going on, revealing that your heart—once a sketchy back alley—is now a well-lit sanctuary. Your new heart isn't just trustworthy; it's fully stocked. You don't need to dial long-distance to Heaven for love or patience. Everything you need has already been installed (2 Peter 1:3). Living out your faith isn't about scraping by; it's about drawing from the endless abundance God has already poured into you.

Deep inside, there's a sacred space where Christ Himself lives—like the holy of holies in the Old Testament. Except now, your body is the temple. And God didn't just tidy up—He gutted the whole place and rebuilt it from scratch, writing His desires on your heart (Hebrews 8:10).

Say this out loud: "I don't really want to sin." Feels weird, right? If you believe your heart still craves sin, there's no hope this side of Heaven. But if you've received a brand-new spiritual heart, then your desires have changed, too. That's why sin doesn't hit the spot anymore. After giving in, do you feel at peace? Or are you left thinking, "Why did I do that?" That internal tension? It's your true desires rising up.

God's not asking you to fake anything. Every New Testament command is about expressing who you already are. Each instruction is like God saying, "Here's how to express the deep desires I've planted in you." It's not about forcing yourself; it's about unleashing what's already inside.

Paul's goal in 1 Timothy 1:5? Love from a pure heart. How could he aim for that if our hearts weren't already new and pure? And Peter? He talks about the hidden person of the heart with a gentle and quiet spirit—precious in God's sight (1 Peter 3:4). If our hearts were still junk, how could they be called precious? Romans 5 says the love of God has been poured into your heart. Ephesians 3 says Christ dwells in your heart. And Galatians 4? God sent the Spirit of His Son into your heart. Does that sound like a place for wickedness to take up residence? Hardly.

Salvation isn't just a heavenly insurance policy to stash away for later. It's a radical transformation at the root of your being. God didn't just tweak a few things —He rewired everything. And He's committed to showing you the deep truth of this new identity. So, go ahead, embrace your new-hearted self, because you're not the same person you used to be. You're new. You're whole. And it's time to live like it.

In the boundless freedom and transformative power of Christ,
Andronicus and Johannes

SECOND THOUGHTS OR SECOND NATURE?

To Liturgical Legalists and Believers Bound by Bunk:

Oh, how you've dazzled us with your theological juggling act—tossing around sin, self, and sanctification with all the finesse of a hurricane in a dollhouse. But now, it's time to peel back the layers of your theological onion, and—surprise!—what's underneath isn't a pearl of wisdom, but a glaring lack of godly common sense.

You've spun a tale as old as time—or at least as old as your grandma's fruitcake recipe—about a grand internal skirmish. A tug-of-war, you say, between the saint you aspire to be and the sinner you secretly fear you still are. This narrative, rife with the drama of a Greek tragedy, has convinced many they're divided beings—hostages to a "sinful nature" that Scripture, when not twisted to fit personal dogma, fails to acknowledge.

Let's talk about the "flesh," shall we? It's not the villainous bogeyman you've painted it to be—lurking in the shadows of every believer's heart like the bad guy in a discount action flick.

(Definition interlude):

> *Bogeyman*: A mythical creature used to scare children—or apparently, Christians. Anything that's wrongly perceived as a legitimate source of fear.

Nope, the flesh is just the leftover programming of your old habits, not some demon squatting in the soul. Galatians 5 doesn't whisper about a civil war inside of you—it declares a victory march, hand in hand with the Spirit.

You've been selling the narrative that our true selves are fundamentally flawed, forever duking it out with a so-called sinful nature. But crack open a more accurate translation (and sprinkle in a pinch of wisdom), and it's clear: our old selves were crucified with Christ. Done. Finished. Toast.

> knowing this, that our old self was crucified with Him, in order that our body of sin might be done away with, so that we would no longer be slaves to sin; (Romans 6:6)

> I have been crucified with Christ; and it is no longer I who live, but Christ lives in me; and the life which I now live in the flesh I live by faith in the Son of God, who loved me and gave Himself up for me. (Galatians 2:20)

We're not some spiritual Dr. Jekyll and Mr. Hyde. We're reborn saints! The flesh is nothing more than outdated software, glitching and popping up like those one of those annoying "update available" notifications you keep ignoring. Let's not get too political, but you could say the flesh is like the old policies of the former administration that still linger even when a new president has moved into the White House.

Misconceptions about the flesh have turned many believers into spiritual navel-gazers, endlessly dissecting every speck of supposed "sinful nature" as if the Kingdom of God is about intense self-scrutiny. Paul, however, points us toward something far better—Christ's sufficiency and the transformational power of focusing on Him (Hebrews 12:2). It's not about the relentless self-examination but a joy-filled journey of walking by the Spirit.

For those stumbling along the way, here's a reminder: while the Accuser's busy pointing fingers, God's even busier extending grace. Your screw-ups don't define you; your identity in Christ does. "You sinned, but that's out of character for you," whispers the Spirit—not to condemn, but to remind you of who you really are.

In your obsession with fighting the darkness, you've missed the simplest solution: turn on the light. Fix your gaze on Jesus, not on sin. We're not called to be ghost hunters within our souls, but light bearers—radiating Christ's love and righteousness everywhere we go.

So let's retire the old, worn-out tale of the divided self. You are not a battlefield for two warring natures; you are a temple of the Holy Spirit—whole, sanctified, and one with Him. The flesh? Just some leftover "stinking thinking." Sure, it'll try to trip you up, but let's be clear—it's not you. You are a new creation, not Siamese twins of godliness and depravity.

One spirit, one heart, one Gospel,
Andronicus and Johannes (two of us, not four)

PART 6

ZEROING IN

WHOLLY HOLY

To the Scriptural Scrooges and Their Desperate Devotees:

Step right up, inhabitants of the modern ecclesiastical zoo! Today, we embark on an exhilarating safari into the wilds of faith, where we'll track down the elusive creature known as "lifeless religiosity"—a mythical beast prowling the underbrush of legalism. (Fun fact: It's not nearly as fearsome as you've been led to believe.)

Let's talk about the Great Divide. No, not the kind that runs through mountain ranges, but the deep theological canyon some are so determined to carve between spirit and soul. Apparently, the spirit gets the VIP lounge while the soul waits outside, shuffling in purgatory's waiting room, hoping for a nod someday. This kind of dualism, as entertaining as a circus sideshow, manages to distort the Gospel and undervalue God's love of every ounce of our being.

Many have wisely tossed out the "sinful nature" myth, finally realizing they aren't stuck with some dreadful duo of "old me" versus "new me." But just when we thought the drama was over, cue the next episode. They've swapped one civil war for another—the spirit-versus-soul-showdown. They find themselves no better off, still embroiled in an internal skirmish of them versus them.

Some have turned this internal conflict into a national pastime, cheering for Team Spirit against Team Soul in an endless game of self-divide. But let's be real—this isn't the Olympics, and there are no gold medals for spiritual self-sabotage.

The Bible doesn't tiptoe around this. It loudly declares that all of us—spirit, soul, and body—is set apart for God. The soul isn't dangling in limbo, waiting for a spiritual squeegee. And as for our earthly vessels? These aren't ticking sin bombs ready to blow—they're temples, home to the Holy Spirit Himself. Pretty posh, don't you think?

To those who've pieced together their identity like a spiritual collage, consider this your wake-up call. There's no split-person disorder in God's view of you. You're a whole masterpiece, fully accepted and fully loved.

Dragging your soul and body through the mud, convinced they're dirty and different, is about as useful as installing a screen door on a submarine. Paul didn't write epistles to some fragmented, tainted version of you—some tiny slice of you locked away in the spiritual realm. He addressed your whole being, calling you righteous, holy, and even blameless in God's eyes. And remember—God's not faking Himself out. He sees reality.

Dispelling the ghost of Gnosticism, let's affirm that our bodies are not our villains. They're not mere shells to be discarded but integral to our worship, instruments through which God's melodies are played. This isn't a call to spiritual liposuction but to holistic health, with body and soul invited too.

To the peddlers of division and purveyors of partial sanctification, we bid you *adieu*. Our identity in Christ isn't a patchwork quilt of mismatched pieces affair—it's a comprehensive masterpiece, fully embraced by God. As we digest this liberating truth, let it reshape how we see ourselves, how we love, and how we live. No longer shackled to the lie of a divided self, may we step confidently into the wholeness and peace of being fully accepted children of God.

Complete in Him, we're not a collection of parts but a symphony of sanctified wholeness. Let's stride forward—whole, confident, and overflowing with joy, glorifying God in every facet of our being.

With our entire beings, we pray these liberating truths set you free,
Andronicus and Johannes

SANCTIFIED, NOT STAGNANT

To the Ecclesiastical Elitists and Their Dismayed Dreamers:

Let's chat about this hilarious mix-up you're sporting—a confusion as classic as mistaking a wolf for grandma. Somehow, you've turned the liberating dance of sanctification into a clunky, two-left-feet affair. Time to untangle this mess with a truckload of truth.

Sanctification is about being set apart for God. It's a one-time deal, sealed with a divine kiss by Jesus Himself. We're talking full access to the holy club, no cover charge, because Jesus already picked up the tab. Have you noticed these verses don't exactly fit into that tidy little "progressive sanctification" box you've been trying to cram them into?

- "to those who have been sanctified in Christ Jesus, saints by calling" (1 Corinthians 1:2)
- "but you were washed, but you were sanctified, but you were justified" (1 Corinthians 6:11)
- "By this will we have been sanctified" (Hebrews 10:10)

Need a few more receipts? Ephesians 1:4, Colossians 1:22, and 1 Peter 2:9, and let's not forget Acts 26:18. These Scriptures aren't whispering—they're screaming the truth: you've been set apart for God, fully and completely. Yes, you—already sanctified, made wholly holy, no assembly required.

Yet, here we are, watching some folks turn this all-access pass into a pay-per-view event. Confusing the sanctification of your person with the setting apart of your performance is like mixing up a Shakespearean tragedy with a Saturday morning cartoon. Sure, our attitudes and actions are getting polished over time, but this doesn't make us belong to God any more than we already do. If God ripped open the sky to return for us right now, not one of us would be declared only 62 percent sanctified. It's all or nothing, friends. We're set apart for Him or we're not. Period. End of story.

This obsession with a "progressive personal holiness" is spiritual stand-up comedy—as if Christ's sacrifice was a layaway plan rather than the whole deal. So let's get the story straight: Sanctification of who we are is a done deal. The daily refining of our thoughts and actions? That's just the Spirit teaching us how to live like the new people we already are, not some frantic scramble to clean up or level up for God.

Understanding this frees us from the night sweats of worrying if we're "holy enough" yet, or if God's impressed by our spiritual progress chart. We're fully embraced, squeaky clean, and utterly sanctified in Jesus. Our daily walk in holiness? It's not a desperate quest for acceptance—it's a victory lap. It's the celebration of an identity we already own.

Let's drop the idea that personal holiness is some slow-cooking project. Your person is holy. You are holy. Period. Embrace the freedom of the Gospel: In Christ, we're already set apart, sanctified, and dressed to the nines in holiness.

Walking the red carpet with you,
Andronicus and Johannes (sanctified as the day is long—and you are too)

LOCKED IN

To the Eternally Anchored and Frequently Flustered:

Rest easy—your salvation isn't some flimsy, here-today-gone-tomorrow deal. It's a rock-solid, everlasting reality. God, in His infinite wisdom, didn't leave any room for doubt: "I will never leave you nor forsake you" (Hebrews 13:5). Not a chance.

Picture God as the ultimate lifeguard. If He saved you from drowning in the stormy seas of sin, only to hurl you back in when you cussed, what kind of lifeguard would that be? Certainly not ours. Our God promises unwavering fidelity—He says, "No one can snatch you out of my hand" (John 10:28). Even when your faith falters, He stands firm (2 Timothy 2:13). God doesn't suffer from mood swings, and His love doesn't have an expiration date.

Questioning your eternal security is like constantly checking your pockets for keys that are already in your hand. It's pointless. When Jesus declared, "It is finished" (John 19:30), He wasn't just completing an IKEA bookshelf—He was sealing an eternal, unbreakable covenant. And this covenant isn't upheld by your perfect attendance record but by Christ's unshakable sufficiency. Your salvation isn't a yo-yo, swinging up and down with your performance—it's anchored in the unchanging character of God.

Is there anything more terrifying than doubting your salvation? Yes—having your faith leaders dangle it over your head like a carrot. It's the oldest manipulation trick in the book: "Behave or else!" We've been hearing it since Sunday school. "You'd better behave, or God's gonna getcha!"

Jesus came to put that nonsense to bed once and for all, but some folks just won't let it die. They take the fire-and-brimstone warnings meant for unbelievers and throw them onto believers. Why? Because they aren't at peace with eternal security themselves.

Here's something Jesus never said: "I came that they might have life eternal—if they can manage to stop being so bad. Look, I've given you a clean slate and a 10-percent grace buffer. Stay inside the lines, and we'll be good. But if you wander off, you're on your own. Are we clear?" He never said that. Not once. Not even James tried to sneak that one in.

Now, let's talk forgiveness—the all-you-can-eat, never-ending kind. Picture this: You're at a gourmet buffet, but instead of sampling bits and pieces, you're handed the entire feast. That's what God's forgiveness is like. You're not partially forgiven, incrementally forgiven, or forgiven on a trial basis. Hebrews 10:14 states, "For by one offering He has perfected for all time those who are sanctified." This isn't a forgiveness plan that needs to be renewed every thirty days—it's a forever deal. Anyone telling you otherwise is peddling a theology as outdated as a rotary phone.

And what about eternal life itself? Not temporary, not conditional—eternal. As in forever. Jesus laid it out plainly in John 3:16:

"Whoever believes in Him shall not perish but have eternal life." Eternal life isn't a limited-time offer. Once you've got it, it's yours. Forever. No take-backs, no fine print.

Now, time to redial the delicate subject of suicide—a topic that's often shrouded in fear and misunderstanding. Let's be crystal clear: suicide is not an unforgivable sin. God is not thrown off by our darkest moments. He's seen every one of them, and He still says, "You're mine." The "sin that leads to death" in 1 John 5:16? It's about spiritual death—unbelief, the rejection of the Gospel. That's the only thing that keeps someone in spiritual death, not a final act of despair.

Imagine believing that God's forgiveness takes away every sin except one moment of deep, tragic pain. That's not grace—that's cruelty. Our God is not capricious. He doesn't revoke His promises because we got depressed. Romans 8:38–39 assures us that nothing—not even death—can separate us from the love of God in Christ Jesus. And yes, that includes suicide. To suggest otherwise is to twist the heart of our loving Father into something unrecognizable.

In Christ, you are fully forgiven, eternally secure, and held by promises that can't be broken. If you've ever doubted that, let this be the moment you finally rest in the unshakeable truth of God's love. And if you have lost someone to suicide, take heart in knowing that if they were in Christ, they are still safely in His arms.

So let's live boldly in this assurance. Our salvation is not a probationary period—it's a permanent adoption. We are His—now and forever.

In the eternal grace and unfailing love of Christ,
Andronicus and Johannes

MONUMENTAL MISSTEP

To the Ecclesiastical Architects and Program Peddlers:

Oh, the splendor of your modern-day cathedrals—the towering steeples, the kaleidoscope stained-glass windows that recount tales of old. Each one stands as a monument to human ingenuity and the almighty dollar. Bravo! You've mastered the art of building colossal temples that scrape the sky and shackle the soul. And those programs! Truly, a chef's kiss to the art of overcomplication.

Let's dive into these expensive church projects, shall we? There's the monumental debt you've racked up to fund them and the not-so-gentle pressure you apply to your flock to foot the bill. You've turned Old Testament tithing into a modern high-stakes hustle. If that doesn't work, no worries—you've got your contracts handy to lock people into giving a predetermined amount. Pretty soon, you'll be handing out spiritual credit scores with a side of guilt.

But wait, there's more! You've even turned membership into a binding agreement—complete with mandatory classes, financial pledges, and a spiritual fine print. It's like a spiritual gym: sign up, show up, pay up—or risk getting spiritually excommunicated. This rampant contract-based Christianity? It's not just a ticking time bomb—it's already going off. Just look at the headlines if you need proof. Instead of nurturing a community of grace, you've created a transactional marketplace, where membership feels like a subscription service.

And the programs—oh, the programs! Professional program-makers have dished out a dizzying buffet of "indispensable" content, and somehow it's expected that we all show up for a taste. But let's be honest—we're exhausted. The blueprint for "commitment" now looks like a cluttered calendar: home groups mashed into service groups, study groups sandwiched between outreach events, and worship nights sprinkled on like some kind of spiritual seasoning. Throw in the occasional half-day retreats just to remind us what peace used to feel like.

Eventually, when relatives invite you to their church, you find yourself faking illness just for an excuse to steal a nap or take a leisurely walk. After all, they'll be too busy consuming their own "indispensable content" to notice.

And let's not forget the sheer volume of activities. Small groups, accountability partners, classes, volunteer opportunities—it's staggering. It's like a middle school lunchroom with more groups than anyone can keep up with. You've turned church into an episode of *Survivor*: outwit, outplay, outlast—or risk getting voted off the island.

But let's get real—beneath the shiny veneer of activity and growth, what do we actually find? A faith that's an inch deep and a mile wide. You've become masters of spiritual entertainment—dropping Easter eggs from helicopters, pastors riding Harleys down the center aisle, and confetti cannons at the ready. People come seeking answers to life's biggest questions, and they leave clutching nothing but glitter and a vague sense of guilt.

Where's the depth? Where's the teaching that tackles the real issues—like: *How forgiven am I? Am I saved forever? Will God ever give up on me? Who am I in Christ?* These are the burning questions that count, but they're drowned out by your weekly circus. It doesn't matter if the music is fast or slow, modern or traditional. It doesn't matter if the windows are stained or clear, if the pulpit's wood or metal, or if there are pews or chairs. What matters most is that people leave knowing the Gospel! Because we all know, that's the real win.

But what we're really left with is a congregation that's burnt out. They're pulled into every group, pressured to volunteer, guilted into giving, and pushed to do more, be more, try harder. It's a hamster maze that leads nowhere but burnout. You've swapped the simplicity of the Gospel for a rat race of religious activity.

Here's the deal: What if we received God's love and loved others as a result? Would we need two dozen programs to achieve that? Or would the Spirit's movement organically inspire us with joy, peace, and love, building community naturally? Maybe it's time for the Church to figure out this new, yet ancient, way of life.

So, here's our plea: Stop measuring success by how large your church is or how many programs you can cram onto the calendar. Go back to the basics. Preach the unfiltered Gospel of Grace. Teach people who they are in Christ. Answer the burning questions about forgiveness, salvation, and security. Focus on depth, not breadth. Build faith, not just auditoriums. Lead people to Jesus, not to exhaustion.

In the boundless freedom and love of Christ,
Andronicus and Johannes

GRACE IGNITES

To the Guardians of Grace and the Pioneers of the New Heart:

We pen this missive to dismantle a few remaining myths that linger like uninvited guests at a housewarming party. You know the ones—they hang around, throwing subtle shade, and refuse to leave. Let's start with the big myth: that grace breeds laziness.

This idea is about as accurate as calling a Ferrari a glorified lawnmower. We've heard the whispers, seen the raised eyebrows. "If you preach grace too freely, people will just kick back and coast." But here's the reality: grace doesn't lead to passivity; it's rocket fuel for passion. When you truly grasp that you're a new creation, it's like discovering you've been given wings—and seriously, who wouldn't want to fly?

The problem, dear saints, isn't grace. It's the centuries-old lie that we're still fundamentally rotten and need a constant dose of discipline to keep us in line. It's like putting a lion on a leash and wondering why it's not thriving. Grace says we've got a new life inside us, a heart that actually craves the things of God—no man-made guardrails required. Sure, trusting this new heart might seem risky, but would you rather spend your life bowling with bumper rails? (Hint: It's not exactly exhilarating.)

You scare the ones who are just starting to lean into their new identity in Christ. Do you know that? Admit it—it's a power move in the religious playbook, like flashing the king of spades in Euchre (or whatever card game you're not allowed to play). It always kicks off the same way, right? "Yes, you're saved, but you're still essentially bad." So unless you buckle down with daily Bible reading, prayer, and the spiritual disciplines, you're bound to spiral. Sound familiar?

And then there are those accountability groups. Ah, yes, the well-meaning attempts to keep us on the "straight and narrow." It's like slapping a fish on a bicycle and getting frustrated when it doesn't' pedal. Accountability groups often come with an undercurrent of guilt, creating more shame than growth. It's a system designed for a corporate audit, not a transformative walk of faith.

James envisioned confession as a safe and authentic act, a place where vulnerability would be met with grace, not scrutiny. But we've turned it into a spiritual weigh-in—step on the scale, let's see how many sins you racked up this week. What if instead, we created true environments of grace where people could be genuinely known and loved for who they are in Christ? That's where the new heart really thrives. It's not about forcing transparency but nurturing a space where authenticity naturally flourishes. Kind of revolutionary, right?

Now, let's tackle the misconception that theological information alone can keep us going. It's like teaching the chemistry of a sunrise without ever seeing one. Knowledge without the experience of Christ's love is as satisfying as a diet of sawdust. Theology has its place, sure, but without the living expression of Christ within us, it's just sterile. Lifeless, even.

Picture a community where the focus isn't on stockpiling theological acumen but on living and sharing the life of Christ. Where laughter and tears flow freely, and joy isn't some rare commodity. This isn't a utopian fantasy—it's the Gospel lived out loud. A child can grasp it, but we insist on layering it with complexities. (Note: simplicity is often the real genius.)

To those still clinging to the old soundtrack, insisting we're inherently bad and need constant correction, please—hit pause. Remind us instead of who we are in Christ, of the incredible new heart inside us that actually wants to express Him. Stop the never-ending recital of our failures, and start celebrating the boundless potential of our redeemed selves. We're not who we used to be!

In conclusion, let's abandon the tired fallacies that keep us shackled to the establishment. Embrace the liberating truth of grace, the power of the new heart, and the vibrant life of Christ within us. Let's live out loud, unchained from legalism, and revel in the glorious freedom of grace and truth. This is the anthem of our faith, and it's time to crank up the volume.

In the electrifying grace of Christ,
Andronicus and Johannes (FYI: No La-Z-Boy chairs in sight)

ALL OR NOTHING

To the Champions of Half-Measures:

Let's get one final thing straight: when God does something, He does it perfectly. So, we've got a choice. Either Jesus pulled off a flawless job, or He didn't. No middle ground. No half-baked attempts. No "good enough for now" workarounds here. It's perfection or nothing.

Now, if we accept that He nailed it perfectly, then three colossal truths stand immovable: we are perfectly forgiven, the law is perfectly fulfilled, and we are perfect new creations. This isn't just some theological tidbit—it's the foundation of our faith.

Repentance. A loaded word that's been dragged through the mud and misinterpreted to exhaustion. Let's clear the air: repentance is simply a change of mind. It's that mental pivot, an "aha!" realization. So when we mess up and sin, repenting isn't groveling for another shot at forgiveness. It's saying, "Lord, that's not me. I'm above that junk. Sin is beneath me. I'm dead to it, and alive to You. Look at me, Lord. You made me new from the inside out, and I'm ready to live like it."

That's repentance. A mind shift, not a plea for more forgiveness. Because let's be real—you can't get *more* forgiven. Jesus isn't climbing back onto the cross just because you had a rough Tuesday. His once-for-all sacrifice was enough. No do-overs needed.

So here's the million-dollar question: How good of a job did Jesus do? If your answer is anything but "He did it perfectly," you're missing the point. His blood was enough—enough to forgive *every* sin, past, present, and future. Sure, there are a thousand great reasons to say no to sin, but getting more forgiveness isn't one of them. Your forgiveness is as complete as it's ever going to get, thanks to His finished work.

Now, let's take a microscope to the Law. Did Jesus fulfill it partially or completely? Some folks love to hedge their bets, saying we're still under parts of the Law. Really? Are you still keeping the Sabbath? No? Then you've got Nine Commandments left, and that's just bad math. Either Jesus fulfilled the Law *entirely*, or He didn't. Newsflash: He did.

Then there's the whole self-denial circus. Are we new creations or are we still dragging around our old selves, needing to "die daily" and "deny ourselves" like were spiritual masochists? Some people preach self-destruction as if it's a holy calling. Let's be honest: if you've got to die to self daily, then Christ's work wasn't finished. But here's the truth: It. Is. Finished. You're a perfect new creation in Jesus Christ. There's no need to kill what's already been raised to life. Trying to "fix" what God has perfected is like grabbing a paintbrush and trying to improve the *Mona Lisa*. Not just unnecessary—borderline absurd.

This message of the finished work of Christ doesn't play favorites with denominational lines. It cuts through Catholicism, Protestantism, and any other *ism* you can think of. The question is always the same: How good of a job did Jesus do? Did He nail it or not? If He did, then we're perfectly forgiven, the Law is perfectly fulfilled, and we're perfect new creations. If He didn't, then we're left scrambling for a Plan B that doesn't exist. Good luck with that!

The Gospel is the ultimate equalizer. It's not about traditions, denominations, or theological preferences. It's about Jesus and what He accomplished. When God does something, He doesn't do it halfway.

So let's ditch the halfway gospel. Let's stop acting like spiritual accountants, balancing sin against good deeds like you're trying to tip the spiritual scale in your favor. The scale has been obliterated. The cross shattered it into a million pieces. Jesus did it all, and He did it perfectly. Case closed.

Let's not miss the beauty of this perfect work. It's not just about wiping the slate clean; it's about empowering the good. You're not merely a "forgiven sinner." You're a saint, a child of God, packed with His righteousness. His perfection doesn't just deal with your past mistakes; it catapults you into a future of victory. You're not begging for crumbs of grace—you're seated at the King's table, feasting on the endless abundance of His love. Time to put down the crumbs and pick up your crown.

In the unshakable, unstoppable, and absolutely perfect truth of
Christ's finished work,
Andronicus and Johannes

EPILOGUE

Well, there you have it: Andronicus and Johannes have spoken. Reflecting on the boldness of their letters, one might chuckle at the tapestry they wove—a blend of sharp rebuke and heartfelt guidance that cuts through the religious clutter of our times.

In this dizzying carousel of contemporary Christianity, they dared to rock the boat. They didn't just entertain; they offered a wake-up call, urging the modern church to rediscover its roots in the radical, life-giving Gospel of Grace. Their words functioned as both a scalpel and a salve, trimming away the dead weight of legalism while soothing the soul with the balm of God's unconditional love and forgiveness.

Their sarcasm wasn't just for effect; it was a precise strike at the heart of the man-made religion that has plagued the church today. They made it clear: the New Covenant isn't some minor update or appendix to God's plan. No, it's a total overhaul—where grace and love reign supreme, unshackling us from the chains of rule-based religiosity.

But they didn't stop at exposing the cracks in the system; they passionately pointed us toward the vibrant reality of a life immersed in God's love. Their message? You don't need a spiritual résumé filled with religious achievements. Instead, rest in the simple truth that you are deeply loved and eternally accepted in Christ. How refreshing, in a world that seems endlessly focused on striving for approval!

Through their letters, we've been reminded of the profound freedom that comes with total forgiveness—past, present, and future sins taken away forever. They spoke to our new identity in Christ, healing us at the deepest level. With a twinkle in their eye, they assured us that we are perfectly clean and close to God forever. No more striving to be "right"; our rightness is a gift—secured by Jesus, not a distant goal we labor toward.

And now, as this journey draws to a close, we're left not with mere amusement or passing inspiration, but with something deeper: the liberating truth of a Gospel that is scandalously free, transformative, and rooted in God's boundless love. The call? To abandon the trappings of faux spirituality and step into the vibrant, liberating truth of a healthy Gospel that genuinely inspires.

This book isn't just a collection of letters; it's a declaration of hope for modern believers—a call to embrace the true message and live fully and freely in God's grace. And we hope you've found more than just words here; we hope you've tasted the refreshing reality of the freedom Christ offers.

What do we hope you've gained? A renewed sense of your identity in Him, a fresh understanding of total forgiveness, and a deep trust in God's love for you. And if these truths have stirred your heart, we invite you to share this book with anyone who you think might benefit from it—friends, family, or anyone longing for grace in a world full of striving.

It's a paradox, really. We bear fruit from a place of rest, because God's grace really works. So, here's to the ongoing celebration of God and a church awakened to its true calling.

Ready, set, grace.

Sincerely yours,
Andrew and John (yes, we know what you're thinking)

THE GOSPEL ZERO EXPERIENCE

A 10-Part Journey for Groups or Individuals

Part One: Covenant

1. According to Hebrews 9:16–17, when does the New Covenant begin? Why is this timing significant?
2. In Hebrews 8:8–12, how does God portray the New Covenant? What are its defining features, and how do they collectively form an incredibly inspiring covenant?
3. What changes did God make with the New Covenant described in Hebrews 10:8–10? What benefits does it offer us?
4. Hebrews 7:18–19 explains why the previous regulation was set aside. What makes the New Covenant unique?
5. How is the Old Covenant characterized in Hebrews 8:13? Why is it viewed this way now?
6. If the Law is perfect, what was the underlying issue with the Old Covenant according to Hebrews 8:7–8?

7. How does Hebrews 8:6 contrast the Old and New Covenants? What makes them fundamentally different?

Part Two: Priesthood

1. Hebrews 7:11–12 suggests God had a purpose in having Jesus born outside the Levitical line. What message was God conveying through this?
2. How does Hebrews 9:15 describe Christ's priesthood and our inheritance? What about those who lived under the Old Covenant?
3. What promise is described in Hebrews 7:20–22 concerning the New Covenant? Who made this promise and what implications does it have for us?
4. How is Jesus's priesthood distinct from the Old Covenant priests according to Hebrews 7:23–25? What does this passage indicate about our eternal salvation?
5. Referencing John 1:29; 1 John 2:1–2; and 1 John 3:5, what did Jesus achieve that the Old Covenant sacrifices could not?
6. Hebrews 9:26–28 emphasizes the number of times Christ died. Why is this significant for our forgiveness and Christ's return?
7. What do the acts of standing and sitting symbolize in Hebrews 1:3 and 10:11–14? What does Jesus's singular sacrifice mean for us?

Part Three: Effects

1. How frequently were Old Covenant sacrifices performed as per Hebrews 10:1–3? How effective were they, and what would have been the outcomes if Old Testament people had what we now have?
2. What impact did Old Covenant sacrifices have on the conscience according to Hebrews 10:3–5? Did they remove sins or merely cover them?
3. How does God view our sins now as stated in Hebrews 10:17–18? What tense is used for our forgiveness, and what does it mean that Jesus will never die again for our sins?
4. Hebrews 4:1, 9–11 talks about a promise of rest. How do we enter this rest, and what provides it?
5. How do we get to feel in God's presence according to Hebrews 4:16 and 10:19–23? Why can we have such confident hope?

Part Four: Law

1. In 1 Timothy 1:5–10, what issue does Paul point out to Timothy, and who is the Law intended for?
2. Romans 3:19–20 reveals whom the Law addresses and what it communicates. What is its effect on the conscience? For whom?
3. Galatians 3:19–24 discusses the Law's message to the world. When were we under its custody, and what purpose did it serve?

4. What knowledge does Paul share in Galatians 2:16? What conclusion did the apostles reach as a result?
5. Do the Law and God's promises conflict according to Galatians 3:21? What can the promise (faith in Christ) provide that the Law cannot?
6. How does Jesus raise the standards in Matthew 5:21–22, 27–29? What was likely the reaction of His audience, and how do people measure up today? What's the solution?
7. Does God grade our efforts on a curve under the Law, according to Galatians 3:10 and James 2:10? How is life under the Law described, and how does it sound to you?

Part Five: Freedom

1. What two effects does the Law have on sin according to Romans 6:14 and 7:5, 8? How do we experience freedom from sin?
2. Who is Paul addressing in Colossians 2:20–23, and what does he say about a rules-based system? Why can we afford to live freely?
3. How does 2 Corinthians 3:7–9 describe the Ten Commandments? What evidence is there that the Big Ten are being referred to, and how is God's alternative for us depicted?
4. Was Jesus born during a period of law or grace according to Galatians 4:4–5? How should this influence our

understanding of Jesus's strict teachings in the Sermon on the Mount?

5. Have Heaven and Earth disappeared yet as stated in Matthew 5:17–18? So, has the Law been abolished or fulfilled? What is the Christian's goal if not to fulfill the Law?
6. When and how did God fulfill the Law according to Romans 8:3–4? What does this imply about our efforts to fulfill the Law today?
7. What does Romans 10:4 say about the Law and righteousness?

Part Six: Grace

1. What role did the Law serve according to Galatians 3:24–25, and what role should it have now that we are believers?
2. How is our relationship to the Law described in Galatians 5:18, and what is God's alternative for us?
3. What happened to our connection to the Law in Romans 7:4–6? To whom do we now belong, and what had to occur for us to bear fruit?
4. What experience did Paul go through to truly live for God, according to Galatians 2:19?
5. Galatians 3:1–3 presents a test to the Galatians. What are the two questions Paul asks, and how do they relate to each other? Should we have different answers for each?

6. What happens to someone who chooses Law-based living as described in Galatians 5:2–4? What standard do they face, and does anyone achieve it?
7. According to Titus 2:11–14, what two things does the grace of God accomplish? Does it sound like God considers a life under grace risky in terms of behavior?
8. Does living under grace render us powerless according to 2 Corinthians 12:9? What enables life under grace to truly work?
9. What did Christ do for us as stated in Galatians 5:1, and why is it important to maintain the purity of this message?

Part Seven: Forgiveness

1. What three actions did God take for us in the New Covenant according to Colossians 2:13–14?
2. How is our forgiveness described in Ephesians 4:32 and 1 John 2:12—in past, present, or future tense? What does this mean for you personally?
3. What do John 3:17–18 and Romans 8:1–2 say about judgment and condemnation? What ensures our freedom from judgment?
4. What two things are given to us in Christ according to Ephesians 1:7 and Colossians 1:13–14, and why is it vital to understand their connection?

5. What does it mean to be fully reconciled to God as expressed in Romans 5:11 and Colossians 1:21–22? How are we described in the Colossians passage?
6. Now that we've been reconciled, what ministry have we received according to 2 Corinthians 5:18–19, and what message can we share?
7. What significance do Jesus's final words on the cross hold for you personally, as mentioned in John 19:30?
8. How does 1 John 1:8–10 address the claim of sinlessness, and what is the solution for those making such a claim? As a believer, have you already admitted your sinfulness and been cleansed once for all? (Consider Hebrews 10:14 in your answer.)
9. Compare the condition for forgiveness in Matthew 6:14–15 with Ephesians 4:32 and Colossians 3:13. Which comes first, our forgiveness of others or God's forgiveness of us, and why is there a difference?

Part Eight: Life

1. What is our fundamental problem and God's solution as explained in Romans 5:12; Ephesians 2:1, 4–5; and Colossians 2:13?
2. What two things did the Law fail to provide according to Romans 7:10 and Galatians 3:21?
3. What was Jesus's main purpose on Earth and God's offer to us as described in John 10:10 and Romans 6:23?

4. What decision must we make to benefit from God's offer according to John 3:36 and 5:24, and what is the outcome?
5. What reconciles us to God, and what actually saves us as mentioned in Romans 5:10? How do these causes and effects differ?
6. How would you define eternal life using John 11:25–26 and 14:6? How does this shape your understanding of the life you possess?
7. Why do we live, and for how long, according to John 14:19 and Hebrews 7:25; 13:5? What impact does Jesus's promise have on you personally?
8. What is most important to Paul in Philippians 3:7–9, and what benefits does he gain from this focus? How does this passage influence your life goals?
9. What good thing might distract us from the most important thing according to John 5:39–40 and 2 Peter 1:3, and how do we genuinely experience life and godliness?

Part Nine: Identity

1. How holy and righteous are you according to 1 Corinthians 1:30 and 2 Corinthians 5:21? How does the 2 Corinthians passage describe you?
2. What does it mean to you to have been given fullness in Christ as per Colossians 2:9–10?

3. What is the significance of being born of God's Spirit as described in John 3:3–6 and 1 John 5:1, and what does it imply about your spiritual nature?
4. What great mystery is revealed in Colossians 1:25–27, and why is it significant?
5. Who are the two "I's" in Galatians 2:20, and what is the difference between their ways of living?
6. What does it mean that Christ is your life according to Philippians 1:21 and Colossians 2:6; 3:4, and how does this impact your daily life?
7. How did sin enter the world as explained in Romans 5:12, 15 and 1 Corinthians 15:22, and what is the cause of our spiritual death?
8. What is our new spiritual location and its benefits according to 1 Corinthians 1:30 and Colossians 1:13?

Part Ten: Growth & Challenges

1. List at least five results of being spiritually placed into Christ according to Romans 6:3–6. How do these influence your self-concept, temptation, and closeness with God?
2. What three benefits of being in Christ are mentioned in Ephesians 2:5–6, and is Heaven only a future destination for you? How does this affect your perspective?
3. What happened to you spiritually at salvation as per Colossians 3:3–4, and where is your life now? What does this mean for your security?

4. What three words in 1 Corinthians 1:26 reveal the flesh's agenda in creating a worldly identity?
5. According to Galatians 3:3, whose work is the flesh trying to complete? What is the solution to this struggle?
6. What does it mean to "put confidence in the flesh" according to Philippians 3:3–6? What was on Paul's résumé, and what might be on yours? How can you shift your confidence to a new source of identity?
7. How is sin described in Genesis 4:7—as a verb or a noun? Why is this distinction important?
8. What does Paul say happens when he sins according to Romans 7:17, 20? How can this understanding help us in moments of temptation?
9. Why were we crucified with Christ as explained in Romans 6:6–7, 11–12? How do we really say "no" to sin?

YOUR NEW IDENTITY

A Scripture Guide

I've been given the right to be a child of God.	John 1:12
I'm born again and can see the kingdom of God.	John 3:3
I will not perish, and I have eternal life.	John 3:16
I believe in Jesus, and I am not judged.	John 3:18
I don't need to thirst for more of Jesus.	John 4:14
I worship the Father in spirit and in truth.	John 4:23–24
I will not come into judgment.	John 5:24
I have passed out of death into life.	John 5:24
I don't need to hunger or thirst for more.	John 6:35
Jesus will never cast me out.	John 6:37
Jesus will raise me up on the last day.	John 6:40
From my inner being flows rivers of living water.	John 7:38
I have the Light of life.	John 8:12
I know the truth, and it makes me free.	John 8:32
Jesus has made me free indeed.	John 8:36
Jesus knows me, and I know Him.	John 10:14
I know Jesus, and I follow His voice.	John 10:27

No one will snatch me out of Jesus's hand.	John 10:28
Jesus is my resurrection life. I will never die.	John 11:25–26
I have become a child of light.	John 12:36
The Helper will be with me forever.	John 14:16
I am in Christ, and Christ is in me.	John 14:20
The Holy Spirit will teach me all things.	John 14:26
I am a branch abiding in the Vine (Jesus).	John 15:5
I am a friend of Jesus.	John 15:15
The Holy Spirit discloses the things of Jesus to me.	John 16:14
I am not of this world.	John 17:16
I am in the Father and in the Son.	John 17:21
I have received Christ's glory.	John 17:22
God's love is in me.	John 17:26
I have been baptized with the Holy Spirit.	Acts 1:5
I am Jesus's witness.	Acts 1:8
I called on the name of the Lord and was saved.	Acts 2:21
I received the gift of the Holy Spirit.	Acts 2:38
I believed, and I received forgiveness of sins.	Acts 10:43
I have turned from darkness to light.	Acts 26:18
I have received forgiveness and an inheritance.	Acts 26:18
I have been sanctified by faith in Jesus.	Acts 26:18
My sins are not taken into account.	Romans 4:8
I have peace with God.	Romans 5:1
The love of God was poured into my heart.	Romans 5:5
I am saved from wrath through Jesus.	Romans 5:9
I have been saved by Christ's life.	Romans 5:10
I received an abundance of grace.	Romans 5:17
I received the gift of righteousness.	Romans 5:17
I reign in life through Jesus Christ.	Romans 5:17

I have been made righteous.	Romans 5:19
I have died to sin.	Romans 6:2
I was crucified and buried with Christ.	Romans 6:3–4
I was raised to newness of life in Him.	Romans 6:4–5
My old self was crucified with Him.	Romans 6:6
I died and was freed from sin.	Romans 6:7
I am dead to sin and alive to God.	Romans 6:10–11
I am not under Law but under grace.	Romans 6:14
I became obedient from the heart.	Romans 6:17
I am a slave of righteousness.	Romans 6:18
I have been freed from sin.	Romans 6:22
I died to the Law.	Romans 7:4
I have been joined to Jesus.	Romans 7:4
I serve in the newness of the Spirit.	Romans 7:6
There is now no condemnation for me.	Romans 8:1
I've been set free from sin and death.	Romans 8:2
The Law has been fulfilled in me.	Romans 8:4
I can now walk by the Spirit.	Romans 8:5
I can now set my mind on the Spirit.	Romans 8:6
I am not in the flesh but in the Spirit.	Romans 8:9
My spirit is alive because of righteousness.	Romans 8:10
The Spirit of God lives in me.	Romans 8:11
I am a child of God led by His Spirit.	Romans 8:14
God is my "Daddy Father."	Romans 8:15
God's Spirit testifies with my spirit.	Romans 8:16
I am a fellow heir with Christ.	Romans 8:17
My body is a living and holy sacrifice.	Romans 12:1
God is renewing my mind.	Romans 12:2
I have been sanctified in Christ.	1 Corinthians 1:2

God called me into fellowship with Jesus.	1 Corinthians 1:9
By God's doing, I am in Christ Jesus.	1 Corinthians 1:30
I have the mind of Christ.	1 Corinthians 2:16
I am a temple of God.	1 Corinthians 3:16
I belong to Christ.	1 Corinthians 3:23
I will judge the world and the angels.	1 Corinthians 6:2–3
I was washed, sanctified, and justified.	1 Corinthians 6:11
My body is a member of Christ.	1 Corinthians 6:15,19
I am one spirit with the Lord.	1 Corinthians 6:17
I have been bought with a price.	1 Corinthians 6:20
I love God, and I am known by Him.	1 Corinthians 8:3
I am gifted exactly as God wants me to be.	1 Corinthians 12:11
God comforts me in all my affliction.	2 Corinthians 1:4
God placed His Spirit in my heart.	2 Corinthians 1:22
I am a fragrance of Christ to God.	2 Corinthians 2:15
My adequacy is from God.	2 Corinthians 3:5
I am a minister of the New Covenant.	2 Corinthians 3:6
My inner man is being renewed.	2 Corinthians 4:16
God gave me the Spirit as a pledge.	2 Corinthians 5:5
I am a new creature.	2 Corinthians 5:17
God reconciled me to Himself.	2 Corinthians 5:18
God is not counting my sins against me.	2 Corinthians 5:19
I have become the righteousness of God.	2 Corinthians 5:21
God's power is perfected in my weakness.	2 Corinthians 12:9
Jesus Christ is in me.	2 Corinthians 13:5
God rescued me from this evil age.	Galatians 1:4
I have liberty in Christ Jesus.	Galatians 2:4
I am justified by faith in Christ Jesus.	Galatians 2:16
I died to the Law. I live for God now.	Galatians 2:19

I have been crucified with Christ.	Galatians 2:20
Christ lives in me. I live by faith in Him.	Galatians 2:20
I received the Spirit by hearing with faith.	Galatians 3:2–3
Christ redeemed me from the Law's curse.	Galatians 3:13
I received the promise of the Spirit.	Galatians 3:14
I am not under the Law as a tutor.	Galatians 3:25
I am a child of God through faith.	Galatians 3:26
I was baptized into Christ.	Galatians 3:27
I have been clothed with Christ.	Galatians 3:27
I belong to Christ.	Galatians 3:28
I was adopted as a child of God.	Galatians 4:5
God put the Spirit of His Son in my heart.	Galatians 4:6
I am a child and an heir through God.	Galatians 4:7
I am a child of promise.	Galatians 4:28
Christ set me free.	Galatians 5:1
I have been called to freedom.	Galatians 5:13
My desires agree with the Spirit.	Galatians 5:17
I'm led by the Spirit and not under the Law.	Galatians 5:18
I live by the Spirit and can walk by the Spirit.	Galatians 5:25
I have been crucified to the world.	Galatians 6:14
I walk by the rule of the new creation.	Galatians 6:15–16
I have been blessed with every spiritual blessing.	Ephesians 1:3
I am holy and blameless before God.	Ephesians 1:4
God kindly adopted me as His child.	Ephesians 1:5
God freely bestowed His grace on me.	Ephesians 1:6
In Him, I have redemption and forgiveness.	Ephesians 1:7
God lavished the riches of His grace on me.	Ephesians 1:7–8
I have obtained an inheritance.	Ephesians 1:11
I was sealed with the Holy Spirit of promise.	Ephesians 1:13

The Spirit is a pledge of my inheritance.	Ephesians 1:14
God loved me with His great love.	Ephesians 2:4
God made me alive together with Christ.	Ephesians 2:5
God raised me and seated me in Heaven in Christ.	Ephesians 2:6
I have the gift of salvation by grace through faith.	Ephesians 2:8
I am God's workmanship created for good works.	Ephesians 2:10
I have been brought near by the blood of Christ.	Ephesians 2:13
I have access in the Spirit to the Father.	Ephesians 2:18
I am a saint. I am of God's household.	Ephesians 2:19
I have bold and confident access to God.	Ephesians 3:12
God's power works within me.	Ephesians 3:20
I have been called to a new walk.	Ephesians 4:1
God's grace has been given to me.	Ephesians 4:7
I am growing up in all aspects into Him.	Ephesians 4:15
Christ grows me and builds me up in love.	Ephesians 4:15–16
I laid aside the old self. I put on the new self.	Ephesians 4:22–24
I have been sealed by the Holy Spirit forever.	Ephesians 4:30
God has forgiven me in Christ.	Ephesians 4:32
Christ loved me and gave Himself up for me.	Ephesians 5:2
I am a child of Light.	Ephesians 5:8
I am sanctified, cleansed, holy, and blameless.	Ephesians 5:26–27
I love Jesus with incorruptible (undying) love.	Ephesians 6:24
God began a good work in me and will perfect it.	Philippians 1:6
For me to live is Christ and to die is gain.	Philippians 1:21
God causes me to want and to do as He desires.	Philippians 2:13
I am a blameless and innocent child of God.	Philippians 2:15
I put no confidence in the flesh.	Philippians 3:3
I have righteousness from God.	Philippians 3:9
I am perfect in Christ.	Philippians 3:15

My citizenship is in Heaven.	Philippians 3:20
Christ strengthens me to endure all things.	Philippians 4:13
My God supplies all my needs.	Philippians 4:19
The Father qualified me to share in an inheritance.	Colossians 1:12
God rescued me out of darkness.	Colossians 1:13
God transferred me to the kingdom of Jesus.	Colossians 1:13
I have redemption and forgiveness in Christ.	Colossians 1:14
I have been reconciled in Christ's body.	Colossians 1:22
I am holy and blameless before God.	Colossians 1:22
Christ in me is my hope of glory.	Colossians 1:27
God's power works mightily within me.	Colossians 1:29
I am now being built up in Christ.	Colossians 2:7
I have been made complete in Christ.	Colossians 2:10
I was buried and raised with Christ.	Colossians 2:12
God made me alive together with Christ.	Colossians 2:13
God forgave me of all my sins.	Colossians 2:13
God canceled my debt.	Colossians 2:14
I died with Christ to the principles of this world.	Colossians 2:20
Rules are of no value to me.	Colossians 2:21–23
I have been raised up with Christ.	Colossians 3:1
My life is hidden with Christ in God.	Colossians 3:3
Christ is my life. I will appear with Him in glory.	Colossians 3:4
I laid aside the old self with its evil practices.	Colossians 3:9
I have put on the new self.	Colossians 3:10
I am being renewed to a true knowledge of God.	Colossians 3:10
I am chosen of God, holy and beloved.	Colossians 3:12
God forgave me (past tense).	Colossians 3:13
I will receive the reward of the inheritance.	Colossians 3:24
Jesus has rescued me from the wrath to come.	1 Thessalonians 1:10

God called me into His own kingdom and glory.	1 Thessalonians 1:12
My heart will be without blame at Christ's return.	1 Thessalonians 3:13
God has called me for the purpose of purity.	1 Thessalonians 4:7
I am a child of light and a child of the day.	1 Thessalonians 5:5
God is faithful to me.	1 Thessalonians 5:24
I have been called through the Gospel.	2 Thessalonians 2:14
God has given me eternal comfort and hope.	2 Thessalonians 2:16
The Lord will protect me from the evil one.	2 Thessalonians 3:3
The Law is not made for me. I am righteous.	1 Timothy 1:9
Christ Jesus gave Himself as a ransom for me.	1 Timothy 2:6
The Lord gave me a holy calling.	2 Timothy 1:9
The Holy Spirit dwells in me.	2 Timothy 1:13
If I am faithless, Christ still remains faithful.	2 Timothy 2:13
The Lord knows me, and I am His.	2 Timothy 2:19
The Lord will give me a crown of righteousness.	2 Timothy 4:8
God, who cannot lie, promised me eternal life.	Titus 1:2
I am pure, and all things are pure to me.	Titus 1:15
The grace of God teaches me to say "no" to sin.	Titus 2:11–12
God redeemed me and purified me for Himself.	Titus 2:14
God saved me, washed me, and renewed me.	Titus 3:5
God poured out the Holy Spirit upon me richly.	Titus 3:6
I've been justified and made an heir of eternal life.	Titus 3:7
God speaks to me in the message of Jesus.	Hebrews 1:2
Jesus purified me of sin once and then sat down.	Hebrews 1:3
Jesus is the author of my salvation.	Hebrews 2:10
I am sanctified.	Hebrews 2:11
Jesus and I have the same Father.	Hebrews 2:11
Jesus is not ashamed to call me His sibling.	Hebrews 2:11
Jesus comes to my aid when I am tempted.	Hebrews 2:18

I am holy and a partaker of a heavenly calling.	Hebrews 3:1
I am a partaker of Christ.	Hebrews 3:14
I have believed and entered God's rest.	Hebrews 4:3
I can draw near with confidence to God's throne.	Hebrews 4:16
Jesus is my source of eternal salvation.	Hebrews 5:9
Great things accompany my salvation.	Hebrews 6:9
Two unchangeables anchor my soul.	Hebrews 6:18–19
Jesus entered the Holy Place as a forerunner for me.	Hebrews 6:20
The Law is weak, useless, and set aside for me.	Hebrews 7:18
I draw near to God through Jesus, my Priest.	Hebrews 7:19
Jesus is my guarantee of a new and better covenant.	Hebrews 7:22
Jesus saves me forever because He always lives.	Hebrews 7:25
God put His laws (desires) in my heart and mind.	Hebrews 8:10
I know God intuitively now.	Hebrews 8:11
God remembers my sins no more.	Hebrews 8:12
The blood of Christ cleansed my conscience.	Hebrews 9:14
I received the promise of the eternal inheritance.	Hebrews 9:15
Christ suffered once to take away my sins forever.	Hebrews 9:26
Christ will return without reference to my sins.	Hebrews 9:28
I have been sanctified once and for all.	Hebrews 10:10
Christ sat down after taking my sins away.	Hebrews 10:12
Christ has perfected me for all time.	Hebrews 10:14
The Holy Spirit remembers my sins no more.	Hebrews 10:17
I am forgiven and don't need any more sacrifice.	Hebrews 10:18
I confidently enter the Holy Place by Jesus's blood.	Hebrews 10:19
I can draw near with sincerity and assurance.	Hebrews 10:22
The blood of the covenant sanctified me.	Hebrews 10:29
I don't shrink back; I have faith and am preserved.	Hebrews 10:39
I please God by faith.	Hebrews 11:6

I have something better than Old Testament living.	Hebrews 11:40
Jesus is the Author and Perfecter of my faith.	Hebrews 12:2
I am disciplined for my good by my Father.	Hebrews 12:7–11
It is good for my heart to be strengthened by grace.	Hebrews 13:9
God equips me in every good thing to do His will.	Hebrews 13:21
God works in me what is pleasing in His sight.	Hebrews 13:21
I will receive the crown of life.	James 1:12
God's Word is implanted in me.	James 1:21
I believe God, and I am His friend.	James 2:23
I am righteous, and my prayer is effective.	James 5:16
I am born again to a living hope.	1 Peter 1:3
I have an inheritance reserved in Heaven.	1 Peter 1:4
My salvation is protected by the power of God.	1 Peter 1:5
My soul is saved.	1 Peter 1:9
I am a child of obedience.	1 Peter 1:14
I am redeemed by the blood of Jesus.	1 Peter 1:18–19
My soul is pure, and I can love from the heart.	1 Peter 1:22
I am born again of imperishable seed.	1 Peter 1:23
I am part of a holy priesthood.	1 Peter 2:5
I am God's own possession.	1 Peter 2:9
I am an alien and a stranger in this world.	1 Peter 2:11
I am free as a bondslave of God.	1 Peter 2:16
I am precious in His sight.	1 Peter 3:4
I have been given a special gift by God's grace.	1 Peter 4:10
God cares about me.	1 Pet. 5:7
God perfects, confirms, and strengthens me.	1 Peter 5:10
I am a partaker of the divine nature.	2 Peter 1:4
I am purified from sins.	2 Peter 1:9
I am called and chosen.	2 Peter 1:10

I am cleansed from all unrighteousness.	1 John 1:9
I have an Advocate with the Father.	1 John 2:1
God's love is perfected in me.	1 John 2:5
My sins are forgiven on account of His name.	1 John 2:12
I have an anointing from God.	1 John 2:20
The Holy Spirit is my Teacher.	1 John 2:27
I am born of Him, and I am righteous.	1 John 2:29
The Father loves me and calls me His child.	1 John 3:1
I am born of God, and I practice righteousness.	1 John 3:9
I have passed from death to life.	1 John 3:14
I have God's Spirit, and I abide in Him.	1 John 3:24
Greater is He who is in me than those in the world.	1 John 4:4
I am from God.	1 John 4:6
I love because I am born of God.	1 John 4:7
I am loved by God, and I live through Him.	1 John 4:9
God abides in me, and His love is perfected in me.	1 John 4:12
I abide in Him, and He abides in me.	1 John 4:13
I can have confidence in the day of judgment.	1 John 4:17
I love because He first loved me.	1 John 4:19
By faith in Him, I have overcome the world.	1 John 5:4–5
I have eternal life, and that life is Jesus.	1 John 5:11–12
God hears my prayers.	1 John 5:14
The evil one cannot touch me.	1 John 5:18
The truth abides in me forever.	2 John 1:2
I have the Father and the Son.	2 John 1:9
I am of God and a doer of good.	3 John 1:11
I am kept for Jesus Christ.	Jude 1:1
I will stand before God, blameless with great joy.	Jude 1:24
I am a priest in God's kingdom.	Revelation 1:6

My name will not be erased from the Book of Life.	Revelation 3:5
I will sit with Jesus on His throne.	Revelation 3:21
I am called, chosen, and faithful.	Revelation 17:14
I am invited to the marriage supper of the Lamb.	Revelation 19:9
I will reign with Him forever.	Revelation 22:5

ACKNOWLEDGMENTS

We are profoundly grateful for the unwavering support from our wives, whose love and patience have strengthened us on this journey. To our families, thank you for cheering us on every step of the way. Your belief in us has been a constant source of encouragement. We love you.

Our church families have provided a nurturing environment where our ideas could flourish. Your prayers, fellowship, and wisdom have been invaluable. We are blessed to be part of such vibrant and supportive communities.

We would also like to extend our sincere gratitude to the technology team that supports BibleQuestions.com, which is powered by OpenAI Nonprofit and The Grace Message. Your talent and tools were an immense help in polishing this work. The recommendations made were essential in bringing clarity to the message we shared here. And to the TGM staff, we say thank you for holding down the fort during the four months we spent writing the first draft. You are awesome!

A heartfelt thanks to Skyhorse Publishing, the Salem Books team, and Simon & Schuster for distribution. In particular, we want to thank Kathryn Riggs, our editor, whose expertise and dedication have been instrumental in bringing this book to life. Your insights and attention to detail have enriched this work beyond measure. We both deeply appreciate your partnership and commitment.

Lastly, we are grateful for you—the reader. If this book has been an encouragement to you, share it with a friend. We thank you for your willingness to explore the depths of the gospel with us.

Reach out to share your story with us anytime . . .

Andrew@AndrewFarley.org
John@JohnLynchSpeaks.com

ADDITIONAL RESOURCES

The Grace Message Radio Programs / Podcasts

- Live, call-in radio program hosted by Andrew Farley.
- On SiriusXM 131 and FM/AM stations nationwide.
- Every weeknight at 8:03pm Eastern (5:03pm Pacific).
- Sundays at 2:03pm Eastern (11:03am Pacific).

The Grace Message, *Good Call*, *Heartbeat of Faith*, and *Bible Questions* podcasts are also available on Apple, Spotify, iHeart Radio, and wherever you get your podcasts.

Books by Andrew Farley:

- *The Naked Gospel*
- *God without Religion*
- *Heaven Is Now*
- *Relaxing with God*
- *The Hurt & the Healer* (co-authored with Bart Millard)
- *The Art of Spiritual War*

- *Twisted Scripture*
- *The Perfect You* (co-authored with Tim Chalas)
- *The Grace Message*
- *101 Bible Questions*

Books by John Lynch:

- *The Cure* (co-authored with Bruce McNicol and Bill Thrall)
- *Bo's Café* (co-authored with Bill Thrall and Bruce McNicol)
- *On My Worst Day*
- *The Cure & Parents* (co-authored with Bill Thrall and Bruce McNicol)
- *Trust for Today: 365 Days of Encouragement* (co-authored with the Trueface Team)

Follow the Authors on Social Media:

@DrAndrewFarley (all social channels)
@JohnLynchSpeaks (FB), @JohnSLynch (IG), @JohnSLynch1 (X)

Get Encouraged in God's Grace at These Author Websites:

AndrewFarley.org
JohnLynchSpeaks.com

Amazing New Resource!

Ask any Bible question and get a biblical, grace-based answer in ten seconds or less at BibleQuestions.com